A NE
OF O

Could Jonny have found his true vocation in life at last? Miss Thrustinne's Sex Clinic for repressed ladies presents the perfect opening (more than one, actually!) and our hero's credentials carry him through the interview with flying colours. His latest job provides ample opportunity for Jonny to exercise his prodigious (you'll have to look that one up in the dictionary) talents by doing the very thing that he's so good at. No, not that thing – the other!
The only problem is: can he keep it up?

The pace, that is. It's a full-time grind and really hard work for a delicate lad. Although Jonny is only too eager to get down to it, there's only so much that flesh and blood can stand . . .

Also in the 'Confessions' series and available from Sphere Books:

CONFESSIONS OF A WINDOW CLEANER
CONFESSIONS OF A DRIVING INSTRUCTOR
CONFESSIONS FROM A HOTEL
CONFESSIONS FROM A HOLIDAY CAMP
CONFESSIONS OF A TRAVELLING SALESMAN
CONFESSIONS OF A FILM EXTRA
CONFESSIONS FROM THE CLINK
CONFESSIONS OF A PRIVATE SOLDIER
CONFESSIONS OF A SHOP ASSISTANT
CONFESSIONS OF A TRAVEL COURIER
CONFESSIONS FROM THE BEAT
CONFESSIONS OF A GAMES MASTER
CONFESSIONS FROM A STRIP CLUB
CONFESSIONS OF A HOUSEWIFE

Confessions from a Sex Clinic

JONATHAN MAY

SPHERE BOOKS LIMITED
30/32 Gray's Inn Road, London WC1X 8JL

First published in Great Britain
by Sphere Books Ltd 1977

TRADE MARK

Set in Linotype Plantin

Printed in Great Britain by
C. Nicholls & Company Ltd
The Philips Park Press, Manchester

Many of my good friends and suppliers of jokes and frillies to yours truly will find themselves listed in the next four pages, with my thanks.

However, this is also a special dedication to the lovely Elizabeth James who has warmed my dinner more times than I've had hot beds. That doesn't sound right. But she knows what I mean. This is for her with love and affection and happy memories.

DEDICATIONS

This is the last lot who managed to creep under my deadline. Unless the economic situation improves that'll be changed to a breadline. Instead of pairs of knickers I shall be asking you all to send me a couple of nicker. Publisher and dirty mind to support.

First the usual thanks to all of you who wrote in. And the usual warning that if any of you have names spelled wrongly in this list, then I'm afraid that it's probably because some of your writing is downright awful. Like trying to read a load of doctors' prescriptions, some of them.

Special thanks to those of you who sent in jokes, and extra-special thanks to those who sent frillies. Remember Uncle Angus and his stall in the market, and keep giving generously.

First dedication goes again to Ann Summers. It's getting to the stage where about half the jokes in this book come from her, so you know who to blame. She sends me such amazingly awful jokes that she makes Tony Blackburn seem like an undertaker on a health farm.

Pandora Varrakalion, sometimes known as the 'Duchess', also qualifies for a special thanks. Not just for clearing out her wardrobe and risking a chilly winter with supplies of frillies for me, but also for her nice letters. She's a great fan of wrestling and also wins loads of competitions. I promised her I'd put that bit in. And also for the following wrestlers, and I just hope I haven't left any out. She threatened me with a submission hold if I did. Or was that promised me as a submission hold if I didn't?

Pandora asks me to mention all the following, and I hope I can fit it all in. A problem that crops up here and there. Mainly there. Prince Kumali, Johnny Kwango, Clive Myers, Count Bartelli, Romany 'Bazza' Riley, Rex 'Sexy Rexy' Strong, Robby 'The Sydenham Sexpot' Baron, Jon Cortez, Kung Fu and Kendo Nagasaki. Plus all his devoted and misguided fans (Pandora said this, not me) especially Chris, Richard and Tony and Kendo's manager, George 'Bird of Paradise' Torontos. Special mentions for Steve 'Captivating Capricorn', Wayne 'Lone Ranger' and Ivan 'The Terrible'. Vincent, known as Baron Cockwell, and I can't actually put in some of the things Pandora said about him. Dooky from Australia. Pandora's cat, Angela, who's looking for a ginger tom. And Eileen who likes John Lennon. And who doesn't? The lovely Liz James is high among his greatest fans.

Nearly at the end. Gary Glitter, Alvin Stardust, Vincent Price, Christopher Lee and Peter Wyngarde. And Hazel, Rita, Jean Williams, Paddy and Chryl.

Whew!

All those men wrestlers. I wouldn't mind a mention for a lady wrestler or two. Or a signed photo to be going on with.

Next there's Janet Collins, who is a nurse in Poole. Good luck.

Then there's Colin Crompton. Still wheeling and tapping. Not to mention shunting. It's nice to know he's a fan, as I'm also one of his.

I suppose I ought to mention Jimi King, who's a DJ from London. But he was very mistrusting about his name not appearing faster than a speeding bullet. But this should mean that all is forgiven. See further on for more on Jimi.

Then there's Jean from Fortrose, and her friends Ann, Mary, Sandra and Heather. She told me all about a visit to the Bay City Rollers but my Publisher won't let me print what happened to them there. But it didn't dampen their love.

Jock Dunlop and the lads from Antwerp.

Phil and Lynn Humphreys from Plumstead.

Robert Brownlee from Sydney.

Carol O'Neill from Letchworth, even though she didn't actually ask for a dedication. There's no escape once you write in to Jonny.

Linda Roughsedge from St. Helens, and her brother Jimmy in the Army. Plus friends at work, Sue, Vickie, Kim, Syb, Helen, Bernie, Deb, Brenda, Dot, Linda, Chris, Keir, Steve, Jean, Phil, Dirty Wally and Mr. O'Keefe the supervisor. I'll save your job for you, Linda, and not mention his nickname in public. Just in case. And with all you birds, not a single pair of frillies! I reckon you ought to have a whip round for me. Or a whip 'em off round.

Joan and Terry Jacobs of Southsea. Hope the wedding went well.

Pauline Spicer and Lesley Clarke who now live in Peterborough but their hearts are still with West Ham.

Hazel and Spud (I think that's his name) of Welwyn Garden City.

Terry Tricker of Ipswich and his mates Hughie and Noel who have unrepeatable nicknames.

Paul Stone from Leatherhead. Got you there, Paul. Actually, he's from FETCHAM near Leatherhead. Fetcham. Right?

Ross and Lorraine Munn of Luton.

John 'n Sue from Sheffield. And don't be ashamed about the team you support. I mean, look at West Brom. Stick with the Wednesday!

Royce Munday of Belfast and Frances. Also Robert and Simon who are two very good friends. I wish I knew what Royce meant about some of my jokes being 'old' in his letter.

Jeffrey Stuart Bell of Bingley.

Jeanne Heavey of Hounslow. And not, repeat 'NOT' the British Transport Police at Paddington. And if they want to know why, they can ask.

Graham Mabbott of Lincoln, and I just hope this isn't too late to impress that gorgeous bird you mentioned.

Dave, Ian, Andy and Mike, who are 'Chiasso'. The best beat group in the north-west. That's what they said, anyway. Also to Jill. And I hope you make it, lads.

John Thirlwall and his sister, Julie, from Sunderland.

Dave Taylor, Tricky Dicky and Mick Slushbag, from the magazine 'Motor Cycle'.

Steve Rennie and Liz Cottam, and I hope the hangovers have finally gone.

Peter Vishnu Smith from Trinidad.

Jenny Longmore (Twizz), Barry Nelson (Basmo) and Karyn Anderson (Kasso). All from Wellington in New Zealand.

Cliff and Yvonne Roles and little brother Andrew. Just to prove that May lightning does strike twice.

Grace and Margaret from Bristol. And I won't make a joke about a pair of Bristols from Bristol. Honest I won't.

Big Mick Hardin from Dinas Powis. And his mates from Shell Tankers, McDuff from McDuff, Ian Jones – Llandudno Taffy, Joe Micky Mouse, Scouse.

Lynda Sheward and Paul Southall. Alias Loony and What's 'is name. Maybe you're married by the time this book comes out.

Brian and Julie, and their three children. Unless there are four or five by now. From Corringham in Essex.

Jane, Allan and Annette Fidler from South Australia.

Chantal Carlisle and Dawn Bell from Newcastle. And thanks for the photo, girls.

Betty and her darling husband John Hibberd, from Framlingham.

Don 'Jethro' Stewart and I wonder if he's still home in Haggisland. And his mates Terry Rodgers, Steve Schleemann, Dennis Pike, Karen and Stella, Doug Price, Spunky, The Woodpecker, Motherwell F.C., Jethro Tull, Barney, Brownie Donk, Jezza, Schultzie, Bog G., Evel Knevel, 'M' and Me. Sorry, that's Don again at the end.

Carlos Ferreira from Cardiff and his friends. Glad I spelled it right for you, Carlos.

Ken Bullough and his wife, Lily. And don't forget what you promised your wife would send me if your names appeared!!

Susan Sutton from Chester-le-Street in County Durham. I hope you keep your word to me, as well.

Steve Kitch Smith from Birmingham, and we all know about blokes who come from there, don't we? That's why he has the nerve to ask if I'm a ghost-writer for some other bloke. Can't recall the name he mentioned. I've looked, but I can't see the Wood for the Trees.

Jeff Briggs of Whitley Bay.

I've just come across (!) another letter from Jimi King. I forgot to mention Gary, Pete, John, Garry II and somebody whose name I can't read at all. Sid and Jan as well. I don't reckon he ever does any DJ-ing at all. Just writes letters to me.

Christine and Karen Robinies, Norman (The best boss in London) and all at C.P.L. And Chris's Mum and Dad.

Wendy Hawker from Dorset. I hope by now you've learned to tell the difference between my books and . . . anybody else's.

Judy Russell from Otago in New Zealand. Who was just in time.

Bob Sangwell and the gang from 'Toosie', which isn't anything rude at all but is just the nickname for St. Osyth's College which used to be at Clacton.

Pommie Paul Cobb, ex of Bradford, Yorks. When he wrote he was in Western Australia. Wonder where he is now?

Ron Hodgson from Western Australia as well, who didn't know about Gillie, Gillie, Ossen etc. etc. etc. Well, he knows now!

Ian Trickett from Rochester, who very kindly made me Honorary Member 44 of the National Worm Racers' Guild. Honest.

Murray and Carol Johnstone from Tokoroa in New Zealand.

Andy Miller from New South Wales.

Dennis Williams and family from Invercargill in New Zealand.

Janet Ann Tomuri from Wellington in New Zealand. One of those pretty tan girls. Although she never sent me a photo to prove it.

Ann Sutton of Fordbridge, Birmingham, her husband, David, daughters Carol and Susan and son Roy.

Philip and Denise of Bristol, who got married just before they asked for a dedication. Hope you're still married.

Ray, Julie and Juliana Doeve from Holland.

Rosemary Sellen from Grove Park. I spelled her name wrong in 'Housewife' so here it is again to make up. Rosemary Sellen. And it was a nice present. Getting worn out by now with use, so if you do happen to have another pair. . . ?

That's nearly it. Must just mention a few old friends myself. Ian and Marilyn; Helen and Charlie; Viv and John; Bill and Michelle. Rob who really does sell jukeboxes, and whose number is still 01–670 6935. Very reasonable prices, and I get a commission on any he sells. I don't really.

Oh! and Messrs. Alcock and Dicks of P.O. Box 244 London SE3, which must be very crowded for them. They have the nicest line in coloured T-shirts I've ever seen. And I get a commission on. . . . Forget it.

That's all for now. Thanks to John Stewart, Doctor Hook, Waylon Jennings and the New Riders whose records have kept me going while typing out this masterpiece.

Last, and least, my Publisher.

CONTENTS

beautiful young ladies. He is covered by more than confusion.

Chapter Seven

There is the first suspicion that Jonathan is attracting a following, but he shrugs this off before finally receiving the royal stamp of approval.

Chapter Eight

It is a well-known fact that there is not actually such a thing as a real live nymphomaniac. But just try telling that to Jonathan May!

Chapter Nine

The mystery follower shows that she has some surprising depths, and Jonny manages to immerse himself in most of them. As with all good books, we end on revelations.

CHAPTER ONE

Hello again! Welcome to the magnificent seventh of my amazing adventures.

What's all this here then? Jonny May a housewife? Has our hero had his testimonials removed from their place of honour? Have I suffered the unkindest cut of . . .

Wait a minute . . .

Sorry.

Opened last year's diary by mistake. I thought it seemed a bit familiar, as the lady said at the wife-swapping party when the lights came on and she found she'd been having it off with her own husband.

Of course, the strange affair of me running a house is all in the past. But even the memory of it causes certain parts of me to break out in a freezing sweat. Like being in an Eskimo's orgy.

Still, how that old diary brings back the happy memories.

(Publisher's Note: When is he going to get in the plugs for all the earlier books like I told him to?)

Now.

I see from my old diary that I have kept the birthday of certain ladies I have known. Pamela Steele who raised my prospects in 'Confessions Of A Shop Assistant'. Linda Loveband who was only the landlady's daughter but she . . . you know. That was in 'Confessions Of A Travel Courier.' Woman Police Sergeant Isabella Hornie taught me that holding a Policeman's Ball can be a lot of fun. That, needless to say, was in 'Confessions From the Beat.'

Stick with it folks. Only another three of these and then my publisher can cuddle up with his inflatable model of the lovely Fiona Richmond and go to sleep.

I've got Brigitte Bartot's address in Paris here in the diary. Bar't'ot and not Bar'd'ot. She was my French mistress in 'Confessions Of A Games Master.' I was going to show her I still care by sending her a French letter, but she might not have understood it.

Here we are. March 18th. Grouse shooting ends in Uttar Pradesh. Well, the diary was reduced. That date's also the birthday of Penny Spendapenie. A lovely lady who taught me some odd tricks in 'Confessions From A Strip Club.' She had some truly cunning stunts. Take care with that bit Mister Printer.

And it seems like only yesterday – come to think of it, it *is* only yesterday – that I was working my fingers to the bone over a hot lady window cleaner in 'Confessions Of A Housewife.' Lobelia Dugfondle. That was her name. And her devil's brood of children. Faith, Bob (as in Hope) and Charity. I give away no secrets when I tell you that the greatest of these is definitely Charity.

I shall now put away my diary and begin this adventure. Anyone who's read so far and likes it, I have to warn you that there is rather more of the naughtiness in this book than in some of the others. So, if you're offended by passages of quite unbridled filth, and descriptions of ladies being undressed and all that sort of thing, then put this back at once.

Incidentally, thinking about naughtiness, nothing much's really changed. My old man's a great fan of the Music Hall. I don't remember it but it sounds like New Faces without the hanging jury. Honestly, some of them. They ought to call it 'Old Faces.'

Anyway, my old man's quite a comedian. He once works in a chemist's for a couple of weeks and a lady comes in and asks him if he's got any cotton-wool balls. He looks her up and down and replies: "What do you think I am, madam? A bleedin' teddy-bear?'

It wasn't a couple of weeks. It was actually a couple of minutes.

I remember. The old Music Hall. He told me about some lady star who told about the time she was walking along the top of a cliff on a narrow path when a man stopped her. "He tried to block my passage," she said. "So I just tossed him off."

At the end of the last volume of my collected memoirs, I'd just caught a train from Withering Bumple station, on my way back to London. And I'm wondering if maybe the lovely Elizabeth James might be back in town and put me up for a few days.

Thank you guardian angel!

Last I hear Liz is off to bonny Scotland with a greasy film director called Luigi Lusta. And that actor who looks like Omar Sharif – to me he was so wonderful. The Italian. It's on the tip of my tongue. Federico Fellatio.

Edgar gives a few hearty twitches at the fond memory of Liz James, and it doesn't take me long to reach her top flat in Notting Hill. And if you want to know, well 'No' her top is not at all flat.

Speaking of Edgar (and who isn't?) I don't reckon that all that washing and cleaning and working away in small dark corners has done him a lot of good. If I hadn't left when I did, then I might have made medical history with housemaid's knee of the Edgar.

Her flat's got one of those peculiar speaker things by the front door. You ring the bell and there's a buzz and a faint voice says: "Burzzzz munglieoped whoogli?"

Ignoring the row of blank faces watching you from the nearby bus queue, you try again. 'This is Jonny. Is that Liz?'

'Querrk ikle di rummmm?'

I start to feel like Dan Dare facing the Mekon for the first time. You remember him? Big green head and the most colossal brain in the known galaxies. Always getting caught by bonehead Dare with tricks that no self-respecting eight year old would try.

'This is Jonny May.'

'Who?'

'I'm May.'

Regular readers will know that this is the most often repeated joke since the tenth showing of 'Bride of Upstairs Downstairs meets the Son of Onedin.'

So let's get it over with and then we can get on with the rest of this naughty tome. Stick with it, there's no better place to be. No place like tome.

The voice on the speaker is not Liz, sounding vaguely Mediterranean. Like the Costa Brava.

'I'm May,' I say again.

'May what?' says the voice with all the predictability of Lord Longdorf – or is it Walford? – objecting to a topless version of the 'The Mikado' on BBC 2 on Sunday evening.

'Not May what! What May?'

'Please?'

'Thank you.'

You haven't read dialogue like this since the last collection of the letters of Bertrand Russell.

'Mister Watt?'

'Not Watt!'

'Nit Wit?'

'Effing May!!!'

'Oh.'

There is a long delay, and a longer silence. I wonder if it might be an idea to make a movie about this sort of situation with a man-eating delay. Call it 'Pause.'

Suddenly, like the last cherry in an ice-cream sundae, I hear the familiar voice of Liz James.

'Hello?'

'Hello, love.'

'Who's that?'

I know the machine's a bit like talking through warm treacle, but I am a little put out that she doesn't recognise the familiar May voice.

'Jonny.'

'Oh. Hello, love. Great to hear from you. Hang on while I get my finger on the button. Come on up.'

The mere thought of a finger on her button is enough to make the front of the strides become pleasantly tight.

I see a sign that says 'Lift' and I try but it's too heavy for me and I take the stairs. But the porter tells me to put them back. I give him a tip – tell him to look both ways before crossing the road – and he allows me to go on up.

Liz lives in a sixth floor flat, and the number, needless to say, is Sixty-nine. A number I sometimes can't make head or tail of. Her bell chimes the opening notes of 'July You're A Woman' by John Stewart, and then the door opens.

'Hello darling,' I say. 'How about a big kiss just for starters?'

'Pees off smiley,' is the reply.

Not from Liz James.

From some enormous and very greasy looking Wop, who breathes garlic all over me. Maybe he thinks I'm a vampire in disguise. If I say I'm Dracula, will he put me out for the Count?

Or will he sing 'Fangs For The Memory'?

'I've come to see Elizabeth James,' I say, bravely holding my ground.

And my nose.

'Pees off beefore I 'it you in bullocks!' replies the ambling Alp.

'You hit me in bullocks, and I kick you in genials,' I reply.

'Pleease?

Well, you can't refuse an invitation like that, now can you? So I tap him gently with the cuban-heeled boots, and he bends forward like some Town Clerk being introduced to the Queen. His face goes an interesting sort of pale green, rather like one of my mum's soups. And I do mean tomato soups.

'Jonny!'

The voice is Liz's and so is the face except for a peculiar excess of eye-shadow. By Sparks and Mensa!! It is a black eye. Jonny is not bad at putting two and to and too twogether and making . . . Err . . . six. Liz with a black eye and a grease-ball with big fists and a nasty temper must have some sort of a connection. And I don't mean the French one, either.

'Hello, Liz,' I say, waving a hand over the heaving bulk in the doorway who is wrestling with his conscience about whether he's going to part with his lunch or not. I step smartly aside as he loses the battle. Funny how when that happens it always looks as though everyone eats nothing but sweet corn and tomato skins. Know what I mean?

'Jonny. Am I glad to see you?'

'I don't know, love. Are you glad to see me?'

She smiles and bells ring with Edgar. 'That's Signor Volare. He's been here for a few weeks as a sort of lodger with sort of . . .'

'Liz. Live like you want to live. It's your life, and you can do what you want.' I could go on like this quoting from pop songs for hours, but Volare is showing signs of recovering and is making noises like a Tory lady M.P. confronted by a male stripper for the first time.

'He's just outstayed his welcome, Jonny, so there's a vacancy . . .'

'I know, and so cleverly concealed,' I come back with the devastating wit that has made me the scourge of W.H. Smiths.

'I keel you!' bellows the wild bull of the pampas.

'Back to spaghetti land,' I say, catching him with a right cross to the moustache, followed by a left jab to the second fly button, which folds him up again like a collapsible table.

The flat is right at the top of the stairs and he sort of accidentally trips over my foot and goes down faster than English football. Trouble with these Italians is that they might have pasta, but they have no futura.

Liz joins me on the landing with a pile of clothes which she heaves down the stairs after Signor Volare, who I spot sitting on the next landing down and trying to hold several parts of his anatomy at once.

'You feelthy bitch!' he screams up at Liz.

'Watch this, Jonny,' she whispers at me. 'I'll get rid of him with a couple of dirty words.'

'What can they be?' I wonder.

'Hey, Gino!'

'What ees it?'

'Work permit!' she shouts.

Aunt Carol – who is Uncle Nick's second wife – once gets very house-proud and decides to paint the bathroom and toilet. They're both in the same room, of course. She even paints the lavatory seat, and forgets to tell Uncle Nick. He comes in that evening and goes straight in the bog, his nose buried in the evening paper. He follows Modesty Blaise, and who wouldn't? He sits down, and three-quarters of an hour later reckons he's finished and tries to get up. Stuck faster than a Building Society to its money. Aunt Carol finally has to call the doctor who comes and peers at the damage. Uncle Nick gets a bit p..d off when the doc starts laughing.

'What's the blurry matter?' says Uncle Nick. 'Haven't you ever seen a backside before?'

'Yes,' replies the doctor, 'but never in a frame.'

Later that afternoon, Liz and I get round to telling each other about what's been happening to us both during the last few months. In my case the adventures would fill several books. In fact they actually *have* filled several books. Liz too has had her ups and downs. Not to mention her ins and outs.

But before that we go in and she makes a cup of coffee and whips up an omelette. As well as being very good at thingie, Liz is not bad at the cooking as well. Not that she could hold a candle to my old mum.

She cooks the same thing, wick in wick out.

Last time she makes a meat loaf, my old man has to take it out after dark in the car and shoot it.

Liz explains about how the Neapolitan ice gave her the black eye for talking to another fellow over the phone, and how glad she is to see the back of him. The coffee has been followed by a couple of brandies, and I get up and kiss her eye to make it better.

I know it's corny, but can you think of a better way to get close to a lady?

After I've kissed her eye, she whispers that her mouth is also sore, so I devote a few minutes to bettering that. Liz seems to be improving and kisses me back. Not 'my' back!

'Anywhere else hurt, love?' I ask.

'Here and there,' she smiles. 'I think maybe we ought to move into the bedroom if you're going to try and make them better as well.'

Can you guess where 'here' and 'there' are? I was afraid you would.

What all this means is that I can either tell you what happens next, or I can say that we go into the bedroom and close the door and . . .

I can't stand any descriptions of naughtiness, myself, and I'm sure that you're the same. So we'll . . . What? No. It'll just be a boring description of a lady removing her clothes better than even Pickfords could. And Jonny doing the same. Then both of us . . . you know.

You really want to read about that sort of thing? Then you should all be ashamed of yourselves. And young ladies as well! My flabber is ghasted.

(Publisher's Note: The gentlemen who sell these alleged adventures have all asked for more spice to be inserted. So please do as you're told.)

I can think of one spice that I would like to insert into an appropriate orifice. Did I tell you about the nymphomaniac farm girl who got all her pleasure from having toad in the hole? I didn't? Then I won't.

All right. Here comes the smut, folks.

The bedroom isn't very big, but the bed is enormous, covered in a blue candlewick bedspread. Liz pulls the curtains and switches on the light on the small table at the head of the bed.

It's got a red shade that gives a pleasant effect. She goes to turn on the tranny but stops.

'Don't like music while you work, do you Jonny? Sorry I forgot, but it's been so long.'

'It still is long,' I reply with my famous charming modesty.

(Publisher's Note: Huh! Mister May would make Muhammad Ali sound like a Trappist Monk.)

I suppose I'd better describe what clothes Liz is wearing before I get round to telling you about taking them off. It'll keep Elias Banglestein of Great Ghoolie in the Shetlands writing to tell me how much he likes it when I mention the word 'Knickers'.

So, here, for Elias and all other lovers of the word, Opportunity is knocking. And the clapometer just measures the amount of the dose.

KNICKERS

Enjoy that, did we? Might even come across some more knickers in a few lines.

First, for the ladies, who love to have details of Jonny's wardrobe. I am in my black tee-shirt. Denim shirt. Denim jeans. Denim jacket. I wish I had shares in Levi Strauss! Black socks and boots.

I'm not sure I want to reveal all the details of my underclothes. I have already admitted that I wear absolutely nothing in bed. Well, if you insist, I will tell you that I wear brief purple pants. There. That must have set many a female heart a-flutter.

Liz is wearing a wrap-over skirt in dark red velvety material, just over the knee. A thin blouse in cream cheesecloth. The cream cheesecloth shows off her gorgeous Cheddar Gorge, giving me a touch of vertigo when I peer down it. Vertigo, darling. It doesn't meant a nasty skin complaint. It's what you get when you look down a big hole.

Like my old mum's mouth.

I'm not saying that my old mum's mouth is really that big, but Evel Knievel wanted to jump across it.

One of the very nicest things about Liz is the fact that she hates wearing tights. Right on! It's like eating a Spangle with the paper still on. So she's got on some black stockings, and dark brown leather boots, with black tops and reasonably high heels.

There's more to come underneath, of course, but we'll come to that when I come. To it.

'Nice to see you, Jonny, love,' she says. 'I have missed you. Really.'

I like to get out of my clobber first, so that the bird can get her fingers on the meat masher straight away. So I drop my gear on the bedroom floor faster than an Iceland flasher. Apart from a slight hang-up when the purple pants get caught up on Edgar who is straining at the leash.

Once that bit's over, then I like to take my time, and I take Liz in my arms, and give her a long, long kiss. Her tongue's busy between my choppers and I'm nibbling on her lips. One hand slides down that gorgeous gorge and wraps itself round one half of her busty substances. My right hand delves under that split skirt, up over the stockings to that marvellous bit of thigh before reaching the borders of the promised land.

She's been shopping in the small ads again, and is wearing one of those pairs of knickers (there you are, Elias) that would make a pocket handkerchief for an undernourished amoeba, and that have air conditioning built in.

My fingers disappear like being sucked into a vacuum-cleaner filled with warm honey. She moans and bites my lips. I pull away, and drop my head lower, unbuttoning the front of her blouse. Nibbling and nuzzling, feeling the cherry in the middle of the whipped cream getting bigger and harder.

Liz loves a tit-bit.

I used to like a reveille. Now I like a penthouse in Mayfair, as long as it's for men only. And of course, for older readers, providing it's spick and span.

The blouse floats effortlessly to the carpet, and the skirt follows it. Hanging on to Edgar like she's a drowning woman,

Liz flops back on the bed, though 'flop' is not really an accurate word. Not fancying heel marks all over my back, I tug off the boots and chuck them in a corner of the bedroom.

My right hand is working away like it's on overtime, and the left hand is doing its own thing (things) higher up. With stockings and that sort of . . . k.n.i.c.k.e.r.s. . . . there's nothing else that needs removing

You may remember the lady mentioned she'd been hurt here and there. Well, I've done what I can for 'here' and now slip nearer the bottom of the First Division, ready to do what I can for 'there'.

Next thing I know there is a great convulsion, like a towering quake, and I'm on my back on the bed, with my mouth feeling like it's full of gooseberry overcoats. I realise now why Liz lives in flat sixty-nine.

Edgar disappears like a container lorry going through the Blackwall Tunnel. If Liz coughs now I can say goodbye to all my prospects. As far as I can tell Edgar is checking her out for any evidence of tonsilitis. Apart from having one of her suspenders digging into my left cheek, I am extremely happy. My mouth is very full, and I am specially involved with the . . . what's it called? A word like chrysalis. Anyway, I'm sure I'll remember it later. It's on the tip of my tongue.

This is the life. You can keep all your money and your power. I don't want any of it.

Not too much of it, anyway.

Happiness is a warm bed and a warm lady inside it.

Liz is rising and falling like the tide in the Bay of Fundy. Honest. It's the only thing I remember from my geography at school.

My mouth is sinking into her passion-pit and Edgar is being deep-throated. It's funny about Liz. She's a very clever lady of the world, but there are times when she'll swallow anything.

I can feel all hands going to the pumps so I wriggle my way out of a tight squeeze, ignoring slight moaning noises from the lady, and make a more formal entrance to this most desirable property.

'Oh, Jonny! Oh, my love. You feel really fantastic. Go on!'

These are the sort of words that most men like to hear. So don't be shy, girls. Let it all hang out. I'm not letting it hang out because it's too deeply buried. I kiss Liz on the mouth, and she responds, driving her hips up to meet each thrust.

It has been far too long (since we last did this together) and I have almost forgotten how good it can be with someone who is happy in their work. I get the left hand squeezing and kneading, blessing the summer job I once have in a bakery mixing the dough for cup-cakes.

Liz's cup-cakes are especially good to get your teeth into. My other hand is on a dangerous mission below the belt, with the five brave warriors attempting to get at the little fortress without being crushed on the way. They manage it, and Liz writhes and groans with gay abandon.

Blimey! Of course I don't mean that sort of gay. Did I tell you about the gay Australian who died in Sydney?

I can feel her fingernails making rake's progress all along my shoulders, and she folds her legs around my waist, locking her heels in the small of my back. I am glad that I remembered to take off her boots, not being into masochism.

It won't be long. Yeah.

Yeah!!

'Yeeeeeeeeeaaaaaaaahhhhhhh!!!!!!'

Don't believe all you hear about oysters being very good as an aphrodisiac. It's not true. I have twelve for supper that very night.

And only eight of them work.

That's the naughty bit over for this chapter, so you can all go and put your kettles on. Or whatever it is you like to wear. I hope my Publisher is happy. Not that anything makes him happy. I remember meeting him once for what he jokingly calls a business lunch. Half of bitter and as many peanuts as you can get out of the dish before the barman snatches it away.

No. I meet him this day and he looks as miserable as the Chancellor of the Exchequer. I ask him what's wrong and he tells me his mother-in-law just drove over a cliff. I tell him that should make him happy.

'Yes,' he says. 'But she was driving my new Jaguar.'

But there'll be several more of these naughty parts still to come. And talking of coming . . .

The next morning, when I am ready to go to bed to get some sleep, we start talking about what's going to happen.

'You can't stay here, love. Nice though that would be, of course.'

'Why not?'

This is like being woken up with twenty penn'orth of wet haddock round your jewel casket.

'I've got to leave in a couple of days. Stay till then, though.'

'I thought you loved me,' I say plaintively, trying to find her soft spot.

'Get your finger off there, Jonny May.'

I've found her weak spot.

'Well?'

'Love is a word that has a nice ring ring to it. Three rings, in fact. An engagement ring. A wedding ring.'

'And?'

'Suffering.'

I do the jokes round here, but as my future is in her hands I keep my mouth shut. Which is more than she is doing. Shaking the hair from her eyes, she grins up at me. 'Listen. I have to go to the Louvre.'

'Well, it's only across the corridor. I could do with a quick pony myself.'

'Not loo. Louvre! I've met this young French film director called Jean-Luc Fromage.'

'I hear he's a big cheese,' I quip brightly, though I feel like someone's cut my toenails off at the knee.

'Well,' Liz says, ignoring my witty interruption. 'I'm off the day after tomorrow, and if you like you can stay here and use my pad for a while.'

'How long?'

'Ten inches.' She pauses. 'So *you* claim. Actually, Jonny, I'm in Paris for about three months. So why not try and get some kind of job for that long, and then we can get together again when I'm free.'

Job! The very name sends cold shivers through my National Insurance card.

'What sort of job?'

She smiles and stops what she's been doing, for which I'm grateful, as it means I can concentrate.

'Funnily enough, I have a friend – a lady – who is looking for someone just like you.'

'Really. What's the catch?'

'There isn't one, love. You have to go and live in her place. It's a big house up in Bounds Green. In North London. Sort of helping out with the patients.'

'A hospital!'

'No. A clinic.'

'Clinic!'

'A sex clinic, Jonny.'

'Come again?' I say amazed and disbelieving.

So she does.

And so do I.

CHAPTER TWO

When she has sprung off to Paris in the Spring, I am left feeling lower than a porcupine's prodder.

Which reminds me of the time that my old man has one of his war-time mates round for a booze-up. I have nothing better to do and the old man's in the chair – which makes a change from him being on the floor.

'Dusty?' says my old man.

'Yes, old man,' replies Dusty.

'Remember that stuff everyone said they were puttting in our tea in thirty-nine?'

'Yerrs.'

'The stuff that was supposed to slow you down in the knockin' stakes?'

'Yerrs.'

Man of few words, Dusty.

'Well,' says my old man, furtively scratching his groin, 'I reckon it's just startin' to work with me.'

I'm sorry to say that's the last we shall see of the ever-lovely Liz James for this little adventure. But her flat gives me somewhere to leave my sounds while I suss out the state of work in London.

Lots of you who've written in – see the front few pages of this book if you don't believe me – say that you like the information about me. Apart from me being handsome and amazingly funny, that is.

So at the moment, I'm playing the 'Willard' album by John Stewart. Dylan's new one. 'John R. Cash' by, well, by John R. Cash. And some of my old Elvis singles. I'm also trying to get into Kiki Dee, but she never answers my letters.

Enough of this music gossip. My brother Morrie reckons

he's keen on pop music. But he's such a miser that I tell him he's starting a new cult. The meanie-boppers.

I can't honestly blame him for being a bit tight with his money, because we don't come from a very prosperous family. In fact, I was a very poor child.

(Publisher's Note: And now he's turned into a very poor writer!)

Ignore him, friends. I'll tell you the sort of bloke my Publisher is. He goes to see 'Lawrence of Arabia' because he's looking forward to the bit with the gamekeeper and the wild flowers. And he thought that Rod Stewart used to be Foreign Secretary. I'm not saying he's out of touch but he did think the Bay City Rollers were a formation dancing team. When I tell him who they really are, he says that he remembers now and thinks they're a load of old rubbish dressed up as young rubbish.

Just proves that even in the worst of us, there's a little bit of intelligence.

I'm telling you about how poor I am as a child. You might not believe this, but if I woke up in the morning without a hard-on, I had nothing to play with all day!

This friend of Liz's has an address up in North London. I'm told that there's a great secrecy about the place but Liz doesn't tell me why. She has rung up this girl to tell her I might be coming.

I was at the time.

Then I have to memorise the address and phone number. Seems she really is running some sort of clinic for people with hang-ups. Or droop-downs. And doesn't want it getting in the papers or on telly.

I don't believe in it, and I'm not going. I decide to try the good old Labour first.

Didn't take long, did it?

I go in and it's about five minutes before opening time, and this old lady behind the counter gives me a look like I'm something she's found on the bottom of her shoe.

'We open at ten,' she says. With that chilling air of superiority I have learned to love.

Still, fair enough, rules is rules, so I go for a walk round the corner and treat myself to a bar of Turkish Delight. Wait five minutes for some Eastern princess to come galloping by on her white stallion and whisk me off to be her lover.

Nothing. Bleeding telly adverts. Should be a law about them raising peoples' hopes like that.

Five past ten and I go back to the Palace of merriment, where there is a longer queue than outside a knocking-shop giving free stamps. The lady and her jolly bunch of smiling colleagues are still crowded in a corner enjoying their cups of tea. No doubt sharing a jest about how they managed to catch some poor woman actually daring to have it off with her lodger and they stopped her benefit for six months to teach her a lesson.

I once go to the Annual Sports Day of the Labour Exchange workers. They have loads of laughs with competitions like 'Steal the baby's bottle' and 'Kick the guide-dog'.

Some of you will be saying why is Jonny so bitter towards such folk? I bet there won't be many of you who've had dealings from the wrong side of their counter who are saying that. Are there?

A lady neighbour of ours back in Brum goes round to ask for help because her old man's left her. Bloke behind the counter looks at her and says: 'Mrs Wobliebumme. You've been married for eighteen years and you have fifteen children?'

'You're right, sir,' she says.

'Well, why then do you want to get a divorce? Is your husband rough?'

'No, sir.'

'Then your husband must be a gambling man, and wastes all your money?'

'No, sir.'

'He drinks to excess?'

'No sir.'

'Ah, then the cause of this breaking-up must be infidelity. Am I right?'

'Yes, sir. He just found out that twelve of the kids aren't his.'

Off on the Piccadilly Line – that's the blue one for map lovers – to Bounds Green and this friend of Liz James. The one who is running a sex clinic, in case you'd forgotten.

Nice little station. Quiet residential area up there. Rows of terraced houses and a few larger mansions. And it is to one of these mansions that Jonny sets his feet.

I'm always quite superstitious and I look round to see if I can spot any omens. The moment I glance skywards I get my omen all right. A face full of pigeon whoopsie delivered from a great height.

Perhaps I should turn round and go back to the Notting Hill pad. Then again, there is a painful lightness in the region of my wallet. I wish I knew what sort of work I was going to be offered. Maybe a sort of consultant being rather a sexpert on the subject of ex. Sorry. Expert on the subject of sex.

I shall soon know.

The lady I have to ask for is Miss Marilyn Thrustinne. And the address is (classified information) which is a rambling house set in a garden that might make a landing ground for Concorde. That is if anyone ever lets old Droopy-nose land anywhere.

Stock-broker Tudor, is what I reckon the estate agents would call it. In need of some renovation. Which means it's right on the edge of falling-down if you slam the front door too hard.

There are great big iron gates like Colditz Castle, with barbed wire along the top. All it needs are watch-towers and that nasty Mister Valentine coming along with a sneer and a scar to drag me inside.

Actually, there's a bell pull. I am afraid of it coming off in my hand. Yes, missus. I'm sure you often have it coming off in your hand. Makes you go deaf. I said it makes you go deaf! Makes! You! Go! Deaf! Never mind.

A lady comes marching along the drive from the house and stares at me between the bars like I'm something in the zoo. Depends how you look at it, I suppose. I might be looking at her in the same way. If I had a peanut I could push it through and see what happens. As she's nearer seven feet than six, perhaps it mightn't be a good idea.

Talking of peanuts reminds me of the time my adorable little sister Melanie got a peanut stuck in her left ear. Old mum takes her to Hallam Hospital in West Bromwich (where the good football team used to come from) and the doctors all have a look. Melanie is actually worth looking at. Finally, one of the skilled men of medicine brings a ladle of melted chocolate and pours it in my sister's right ear.

The peanut came out a Treat!

The giantess opens her mouth. 'Yes?'

Her voice is as deep as the ocean and as wide as the sky.

'I'm Jonathan May and I've been asked to come along here and see Miss Thrustinne.'

'Will you come inside?' says the lofty lady.

'If you provide me with a step ladder,' I quip.

Many a quip 'twixt whatever it is.

She takes a key off her ring (?) and unlocks the main gate, holding it open just long enough for me to slip through, then slamming it closed again, turning the key in the lock with the sort of finality I associate with Vincent Price and damp crypts.

Crypts are always damp. Must be the cats that creep in the crypt, crap and creep out again.

'Will you walk this way?' asks Gargantua, striding out up the drive towards the ivy-covered walls of the house.

'If I could walk that way, I wouldn't need the talcum powder,' I reply, carefully pitching my voice low enough for her not to hear.

I am shown into a room rather like a dentists' waiting-room. Picture of the stag at bay and a pile of old magazines. Mainly 'Punch', 'Telegraph' supplements and 'Woman'.

Thinking of the stag at bay reminds me of a teacher at my old junior school. Not exactly in the heart of the country, it wasn't. We have this new teacher who shows us pictures of all sorts of animals, including this great big deer with a fine spread of antlers.

'What is this?' she asks us.

Nobody answers. Co-operating with the enemy that would be.

Waving the deer around, she tries again from a different angle. That sometimes works, doesn't it fellows?'

'This picture. It's name is the same as the name your mummies sometimes call your daddies.'

Up goes the hand of Pigmeat Packham. 'Miss. I know. And I always wondered what a horny bastard looked like.'

There is a bit of crackling in the air, like passing a pork factory, and a disembodied voice comes from a small speaker in the corner of the waiting room. 'Will Mister Hay go to Room Sixty-nine on the second floor.'

That number again.

I put down an exciting article about 'The Most Forgettable Character I Never Met' and walk along a corridor and up a flight of stairs. I'm not saying that the stairs were very large, but I wouldn't have been surprised to meet Jimmy Cagney on the way up dancing to 'Yankee Doodle Dandy'.

That reference is for the grandparents among my readers.

Room sixty-nine has a heavy oak door painted the sort of pink I always associate with ageing lady novelists. There is a small sign that says: 'Knock and Enter'.

I do both.

Actually I only knock, because when I try to enter I find

the handle is stuck. I grab hold of it and give it a good old pull. It's often the only way, isn't it missus?

Only to find that there is someone pulling the other way from the other side.

'Let go! I'll unlock it!' calls the voice.

I do and notice there is some fluff on my right trouser leg. There is a rattling from behind the door as though the person there is having trouble. So I take a chance and lean on the door to brush myself down.

With predictable Jonny May luck, the door chooses that moment to be opened and I am catapulted across the threshold, landing flat on my handsome face in six inches of luxurious pile.

The lady who has opened the door – for it is a she – sniffs like she has a nasty cold.

Incidentally. Never rub noses with a promiscuous Eskimo. You might catch sniffilis.

'Sorry,' I say, without looking up. 'I'm always falling for ladies.'

'Indeed. Most amusing.'

The temperature inside the room drops to sub-Arctic levels.

'Please get up and sit down, Mister Hay.'

'I'm May.'

'There is no may about it, Mister Hay. While you are here you will do what I tell you.'

I finally lift my head from the carpet and look at this chilly lady.

By Isaac and Asimov!

The temperature in the room rises again faster than support for the Scottish Nationalists. She is a lovely lady indeed. And in thought for all I know.

Not far off six feet tall, with long honey-blonde hair cascading over her shoulders like a rain of golden wheat. Aaah, isn't that lovely! Blue eyes as clear as the summer sea off the sunshine resort of Biggrippov. Figure that shows in all the right places. Dress of maroon corduroy over bare legs and patent leather shoes.

'Will you do as you are told, Mister Hay.'

Perhaps she's going to try and force me. I like a battle of wills. And testaments. The weather looks bright through the window, so it occurs to me that she might try to make Hay while the sun shines.

'I'm not Hay I'm May.'

'I'm sorry.'

'Not Hay, May.'

'Not Hymie who?'

'Not Hymie anyone. Nor Hay. Nor Bad. Nor Good. Nor Wood. Nor anything like that. Jonathan May.'

At last her face creases a little at the edges in what I suss out is the best she feels like doing in the smile area.

'I understand. When Liz told me about you the line wasn't all that good. I felt that I couldn't keep asking her to come again.'

'I know precisely what you mean,' I reply, my face straighter than a judge's morals.

'Did Liz tell you anything about our work here?'

'She said that it was very secret and that you didn't want to get in the papers or on the box.'

'Yes. That is true. You've told nobody that you're here?'

'Sot a noul.'

'What?'

'Got a hole. Damn! I mean not anybody.'

'Good. I am trying to set up here in London an inter-personal relationship centre for those suffering from intimate sexual problems.'

'Sex clinic?'

'Well, more or less. But I don't like the phrase. All our patients will maintain the strictest anonymity. Is that quite clear, Mister May.'

'Jonny. And yes, it's all as clear as can be.'

It occurs to me that I haven't mentioned that I have actually risen from the floor and am now sitting in a comfortable chair the other side of a desk from the lady. That's in case any nits among you thought I was carrying on this conversation from flat on my face!

She is wrestling with the drawer of the desk, which seems to be stuck fast. Or stuck slow if you prefer. Please yourself.

'You must be Marilyn?'

'I'm thrusting.'

'Try lifting as well,' I suggested helpfully.

'That is my name. Miss Thrustinne.' She gets her drawers unstuck and becomes more friendly. I've noticed that with other ladies. Get their drawers unstuck and they're anybody's. 'But you may call me Marilyn. In front of patients, I shall refer to you as Jonny. And you will not use my surname at all. It helps to maintain confidentiality. The patient doctor relationship. Sacrosanct.'

Sacrosanct! Don't know what that means. Sounds like a report on a Japanese shipping disaster.

I am quite looking forward to doing some work under the lovely Miss Thrustinne. But what kind of work can it be?

'Marilyn?'

'Yes, Jonny?'

'Will I be living in?'

'Yes. There is accommodation on the top floor of the west wing. Next door to mine.'

'Aye, aye!' I hear some of you go. Dirty devils you are.

'That's fine. Not haunted I hope?'

'No. But parts of the building are supposed to be infested with spirits.'

'Ninety per cent proof, I hope.'

'Not funny, Jonny.'

'I've brought my spirit-level.'

'Even more not funny. I'm very busy as our first patients should be coming soon, and I want to be ready.'

You think I'm going to make yet another joke about 'coming' don't you?

(Publisher's Note: Yes.)

There are few greater pleasures in life than being able to disappoint my Publisher. He's supposed to be very shrewd you know. But I doubt it. The last two books he published were those lengthy volumes: 'The Brummie Book of General Knowledge' and 'Mountain Climbing in Holland'.

'Right, Jonny. Let's get on with a short interview. Age? I said how old are you?'

'Old enough to know how and not too old not to be able to do it.'

'Good.'

She's not joking. I make the joke and she calmly writes it down. I have never had this sort of interview. When is she going to start asking about my previous employers and the positions I held at school? Not including the missionary position. Interests and hobbies. Eight references from vicars and lawyers and all that crap.

'You're healthy?'

By Brush and Basil! Just what sort of job is this going to be? She'll be asking if she can take down my particulars next so that she can examine my credentials!

'Jonny. Will you take down your trousers so that I can examine your genitals.'

'Ha, ha, ha, ha, ha. Haaaaaaaaaaa!'

CHAPTER THREE

I lay my hand on my heart and promise you, that is exactly what Miss Thrustinne says to me. Calm as you like. Sitting there, her lips parted expectantly.

I wouldn't have minded, but she pulls out a twelve inch steel ruler.

'Don't you touch me with that!' I squeak. Well, I remember the teacher in my infants' school used to have a ruler like that and she carried it constantly. Lovely lady. Would have made a good Commandant at a concentration camp. She had ways of making you concentrate. Like belting you over the clenched knuckles with the edge of the ruler.

Marilyn smiles. 'Don't be silly. It's only to measure you with. You need a minimum length for therapy work with lady patients.'

At last the new pee has dropped. All over the floor, with a resounding tinkle.

That's the job!

Doing thingie with lots and lots of frustrated ladies. All day long. And all night short. In and out and getting paid for it. I can't believe it. Thank you, guardian angel. Thank you. Thank you.

At last, I've found the ideal job. Something that I can do superbly well. And never get bored. I'm sorry to disappoint you fans, but I'm afraid that this is going to be the last of my adventures. I don't reckon I shall ever need another job. Happiness for ever and ever.

(Guardian Angel's Note: He really should learn, shouldn't he?)

'Come on, Jonny. Drop them.'

All of a sudden I come over all shy. I don't mind stripping

for a doctor. Or if it's in connection with making a connection. But not in front of this very cool and attractive lady. I can feel Edgar making desperate efforts to hide away in the strides.

'Not going soft are you, Jonny?'

'Blimey!' She must have X-ray eyes.

Which reminds me of a time I'm sitting in the park, just watching the conkers grow. I prefer female conker trees. They have nicer limbs and no nuts.

There's this little girl sitting next to me, crying her heart out. I am about to be a good Samaritan when an old man of about sixty comes and sits next to her, and touches her on the shoulder.

I watch him, ready to call a constable. I haven't decided what I'll call him, so I listen.

'What's wrong, little girl?'

Sob, sob, sob, she goes. As though her heart is broken.

'Come now. There is nothing in the world that is worth crying about like that. Is there?'

'It's my brother Antony.'

'What about him?'

'He's ten years old. And I want what he's got and I can't ever have one and that's why I'm crying.'

'I tell you whatever it is your brother's got, it's not worth crying about.'

'But I want one. It's a thing that goes hard and stands up. Then he makes it go soft. Then it goes hard and stands up. Then he makes it go soft. Then he makes it go hard and it stands up again. Then . . .'

At this point the old man bursts into tears.

'Mmmm. Not bad. Certainly rather above the figures that I had in mind.'

Standing there like a bottomless waiter while this lovely lady takes Edgar in hand puts my mind to her figure. And the more I think about how her supercargo is almost bursting out of her dress, the . . .

'Well! That's even better. My goodness, Jonny. That's something to be proud of.'

What have I been telling you for the last six books? Of course it is. Even the rather chilling touch of the steel ruler doesn't deter it.

Edgar is definitely not deterred. Nor is he de second. He is de first!

'Are you sure you don't need a longer measure, Marilyn? It looks from up here as though . . .'

She must have been a nurse. There's a technique where you flick the end with your index finger and everything shrinks quicker than . . . I can't think of anything that shrinks faster than Edgar when someone flicks him on the end with their index finger!

'Get dressed again, Jonny. I've a few questions to put to you. Of course they will be rather personal, but I'm sure that won't worry you at all.'

'No. No, fire away.' I pull up my jeans while she sits down again behind the desk and pulls out an enormous red folder. Reading upsidedown, I see the words: 'Personal File of Male Therapist.'

Hereapist, thereapist, everywhereapist!

Needless to say, that reminds me of a little joke. After retailing it to you, I shall come back to the questions that Marilyn asks me.

I'm out in a car with my brother Morrie. I know that those mean skinflints at Heinz never sent me any tins of tomato soup despite all the free plugs I give them, but it's worth trying again for a car.

Morrie is driving a Volvo at the time of this tale. Well, if I'm actually honest, it isn't a Volvo. It's just that I rather fancy a free Volvo. Morrie is driving a more common British car.

It breaks down.

Pouring with rain, and we're miles from anywhere, when we hear singing coming through the night and this staggering drunk comes lurching into view.

'Hello, hello, hello!' he calls. 'Wassermatter! Wash wrong with thish car?'

Morrie is not noted for his tolerance of others, unless they happen to have a lot of money. He barks over his shoulder: 'Piston broke.'

'Thash funny,' mumbles the drunk. 'So am I.'

Marilyn slips on a pair of glasses. I once slipped on a large cow-pat, but that's a different story. King Pong.

'Ready Jonny?'

'Ready.'

'In an oral-genital pre-copulatory situation, with a one-to-one ratio, providing that fellationary activity is satisfactory, giving a nine point five on a ten scale, for how long would you provide clitoral massage before prolonging lingual friction of the labia?'

'Yes.'

'What do you mean, "Yes"? That's no answer.'

'It is when you don't understand the question, Marilyn. Can we try another? Maybe I'll do better. If you've got any that are in English, I might improve.'

'Tut, tut.' I've never actually heard anyone say that. Seen it written down, but never heard it. She adjusts her spectacles, and crosses her legs. The desk has one of those cutaway bits for your legs, and as I bend down to zip up my boots I can't help catching a glance of Miss Thrustinne's legs. And what lies at the top of them. It's hard . . . to see, but I could swear that she is wearing some kind of furry knickers. Unless . . . but no lady would go around without any on at all.

Would she.

I knock a pencil on the floor just to check it out.

She would.

'Are you all right, Jonny?'

'Yes. Yes, thanks.'

'Only your face has gone rather florid.'

'My mum likes my face. And I could quote you plenty of ladies who didn't think my face was horrid.'

'Florid. But let it pass. Here's another question. In sado-masochistic ritualism, with coprophiliac overtones, does the concept of circulatory compression with bondage suspension and total subservience find a response in your psyche?'

I swear this is what she says. I don't know whether any of you can make anything of it, but I certainly can't. She sees me looking blanker than a warehouse wall and puts the folder down.

'These are simple questions to find out the level of your sexual experience and to what limits you're prepared to go to help in our work.'

I see a glimmering of light, like a match at the end of a railway tunnel.

'Ah. You want to know how often I've had it. How good I am at it. And what I think about it?'

She nods. 'More or less. Yes.'

'I've said this before, Marilyn, but when I meet a lady that I fancy and that I reckon fancies me, then there are only two simple questions. "Do you like it?" and "Do you want it?" If both questions get a smile and a wink, then I know I'm home and . . . dry. So to speak.'

'I see. And you have found that this . . . rather elementary system works well enough for you?'

'Yes. I've had my share of what's going.'

Marilyn gets up and walks slowly round the room, sucking the end of a felt-tip pen in a way that makes me wonder how my tip felt. And the answer is that it feels rather well, thanks a lot.

'Try it.'

'What?'

'Try it on me. Your method.'

'Don't be silly.'

'Why not?'

'It's like saying that I'm going to pick your pocket by

pointing out of the window. When I try it, you won't look out of the window because you'll know it's a trick.'

'And?'

'And I won't prick your poxit. Sorry. Pick your pocket. So, the answer is not in the affirmative.'

I'm pleased with that one. I used to watch that Irish bloke who did 'What's My Line?' for about fifty years. The one who made that record of 'Shifting, Whispering Sands!' And that should stir a memory or two among the housewives who find me choice.

They used to say things like: "Would I not have been about to have been right if I had not surmised that you might not be wage-earning?"

Looking back, it makes you wonder why it was so popular, doesn't it? When you compare it to modern chart-toppers like Nicholas Parsons. My old mum loves him. Says he reminds her of a Christmas turkey. Because when he gives them the answer, she shouts: 'Parsons knows. Parsons knows.'

Marilyn comes and sits down on the edge of the desk, right by me, and kicks off her shoes, putting her bare feet on my lap. Edgar has no objection to being down-trodden in a good cause, and begins to rise to the occasion. Sitting like that I am able to confirm my previous suspicions about the underwear. Lack of underwear.

'Jonny,' she says, giving Edgar the benefit of her soul. Soles. Which makes me feel a bit of a heel. Bits of both her heels. Something is definitely a'foot.

'Yes,' I squeak, wondering why my voice has suddenly got rather out of control.

'I know how you're going to try and do it. But I'd still like to see it. At first hand, so to speak.'

It is not her hands that are worrying me.

'It's important to know that you're good enough to trust with some very important patients. Suppose when it came to it, and you couldn't even raise a smile.'

I raise a smile.

'Go on, then.'

'I'm not sure this is the time or the place, Miss Thrustinne.'

'Marilyn.'

'Marilyn.'

'Let me help a bit. You look rather cramped.'

Before you can say 'Chelsea are rubbish', she leans forwards, so that my lap is buried under that veil of golden hair, and undoes my zip. Cool fingers are inside my under-strides, and Edgar is out in the open air.

'There.'

She sits back again, running her toes up and down the pork prodder. There have been birds I wouldn't fancy doing that to me. Some of them have feet like paving-slabs.

But Marilyn has lovely feet and it is a pleasure. Since she wants me to try my unfailing system, then I suppose I'd better. Those of you who've followed me through my many adventures will know that I am actually shooting the lady rather a line, as such an approach is not my style. But as I've made my bed, then I must sleep in it. Though sleeping is the thing furthest from my mind. Thingie is closest to my mind.

'All right.'

'I'm ready. Isn't it warm in here, Jonny? Have you noticed?'

Boggle, boggle, I go. Marilyn undoes the front of her dress, so that it falls right back over her shoulders, revealing as fine a pair as these eyes have ever seen. Firm and big and pointed. I worry in case she turns round without warning and takes my eye out.

'Right. Marilyn. Do you like it?'

'What's it?'

'It. Thingie. You know?'

'Copulation? Intercourse?'

I hate women who talk dirty, and nearly jack the whole thing in. But those knockers are hypnotic.

'Yes. Do you like it?'

'Yes. I love it.'

If the foot massage goes on much longer I am going to leave

the room with a stain on my character. Or at least one on the carpet.

'Then, do you want it?'

'Yes. Right away.'

Caught you there, didn't I?

Actually, there is a small pause between the asking the question and her answering. And the intercom buzzes. She picks it up and says: 'Yes. Right away.'

Get it?

More than I do.

Really reckoned my chances there. Reminds me of the Brummie who goes down to London and goes in this club. He tells his mates about it afterwards.

'Lovely girl,' he says. 'Invites me up to her room after the club closes. Red light in the window. Says she's a model. Smashing bit of crackling. Asks me if I want a cup of tea, and I say I do. Tells me to take my clothes off and relax, but I'm shy. Doesn't stop her. Peels off the lot. Lies on the bed smiling at me. Then I ask her what about this cup of tea. She gives me a funny look and tells me it'll be eight pounds. Too bloody much I reckon for a cup of tea. I'm not stupid, you know. So I walk out. But . . . I reckon that if I'd played my bleeding cards right there I could have stuffed her.'

'Jonny. Please do up your trousers and compose yourself. Our first patient has arrived.'

Compose yourself! Who does she think I am? André Prevert? Just when I reckon I'm in the home straight, and that has to happen. Still, if I'm going to be living here and working away with loads of lovely frustrated ladies, then there will still be time to give Miss Thrustinne the benefit of my quite unique form of central heating.

By the time I've got myself zipped up, taking extra care not to nip Edgar in the buds, Marilyn is sitting back behind her desk, looking like butter wouldn't melt in her mouth. The thought of that luscious mouth running with hot sticky butter is almost too much for Edgar and he makes a determined effort to break out of my maximum security underpants.

'Remember, Jonny. Treat this establishment as a proper hospital. And keep your mouth shut tight.'

'Mmmmeeerrruummmm!'

'What?'

'That was me talking with my mouth shut.'

'Very droll. Merriment and what-not! Keep your mouth shut except when you're using it for something important.'

There goes Edgar again!

Actually, hospitals always make me feel ill. A mate of mine called Tiny Terry Parknett (Tiny because he's not) goes into this hospital for a gall bladder operation. Says to the doctor: 'After this operation, will I be able to power my way around making love to my girl friend?'

'Of course,' replies the doctor, anxious to get off and start his day's work on the golf course.

'Great!' says Tiny Terry. 'She wouldn't let me do it before.'

Before I meet the new arrival, Marilyn fills me in, though I'd rather it had been the other way round, on what my duties will be. Where I live. Nice little room on the top floor. What my hours are. When I'm needed, but she urges me to be flexible. (!)

Wages. They're a secret between the taxman and me, but there are certain perks and free meals and that sort of thing. Not to mention that sort of thingie.

'Most of the ladies you'll be trying to help, will have some kind of deep-rooted sexual problem. Some will have repressions.'

'Like on the weather,' I chirp brightly, to show I'm paying attention.

'What?'

'A deep repression centred over Iceland.'

'Quite.' A deep depression settles over the room. Marilyn

sits back and taps a pencil on her desk. 'You know, Jonny, despite the high recommendation from Elizabeth James, I'm frankly not convinced you are quite the right sort of personality to cope with this position.'

I see free bawds and lodging slipping away and make an effort to grab them back.

'I can cope with any position. Honest. I've studied the 'Calm Yer Hooter' and 'The Gold In The Aston-Martin.' So you see I . . .'

'What is "The Gold In The Aston-Martin"?'

'Oh. I think I mean "The Jewel In The Lotus." Sorry. But I honestly will try to do my best.'

'But will you be good?'

I resist the temptation to say that I will be really terrific and simply nod my head looking modest.

'Very well. The first patient is Mrs. Arturia Legend. You may take her out up to town for the afternoon and show her around. Help her relax and get her ready for the first session of therapy tomorrow morning. Can you do that?'

'Yes. Two questions. What's wrong with her?'

'Confidential. Nothing that you should have any problem in handling. Second question?'

'Can I have some money?'

'Of course. Call at the office and ask Miss Tanner for some.'

'Shouldn't that be Miss Two-And-A-Half New Pence?' I get a glare to freeze the seedpods off a polar-bear and walk to the door, glad that Edgar has temporarily given up struggling for freedom.

'Jonny?'

'Yes?'

'Tact and patience and diplomacy. Remember all those three things.'

'You can rely on me,' I say, walking confidently into a store cupboard.

Mrs. Arturia Legend is waiting for me when I come out of

the office folding a bunch of crisp fivers into my wallet. She is about forty, and looks as sweet and innocent as a Sunday School teacher. Black dress that covers her from neck to below the knee. Small woollen hat. Sensible shoes. Black handbag. Black woollen gloves that she's nervously playing with.

I wonder what her problem can be?

We introduce ourselves and walk down the shaded drive, past the Amazon on the gates. And stroll quietly towards the Tube Station.

'Right, then, Mrs. Legend. Where shall we go and what would you like to do?'

She smiles up at me as demurely as if she were taking tea with the Vicar. 'I'd like to go somewhere very public and very crowded.'

I am rather puzzled. But I'm paid to do what she wants. 'Fine. Then what would you like?'

'Then . . . then I'd like you to roger me rigid!'

CHAPTER FOUR

To give you time to get over that shock, I'll just mention again the idea of writing to me, c/o Sphere Books, at 30-32 Gray's Inn Road, London WC1. Anyone who writes in with jokes before Easter 1977 will get a mention in the Dedications pages of one of my latest adventures. And there's also a small competition. The person who sends in the best jokes will also win *ten pounds* and a *special* mention.

I don't mind naughty jokes, but not actually dirty ones. If you've read enough of my books, then you'll have a rough – very rough – idea of what I mean. And no racial jokes because I don't like them. And I'm the judge. One of them, anyway. If any ladies think that sending me naughty pictures of themselves or pairs of frillies will help them to win a prize, then I'm not going to put them off by saying they're wrong. Of course, I'm not actually saying they're right, either.

Doesn't matter if they're old jokes. Long ones or short ones. All the same to me. I'll give you an idea of the sort of joke I like.

My Uncle Angus wins this competition, the first prize of which is a night out with all of Pan's People. Lucky Uncle Angus! I say that. But Uncle A.'s worried about how he'll be able to cope with such a handful of luscious lovelies. And if they ever get to read this I wouldn't mind a signed photo.

So he goes to the doctor and tells him his worry. The medicine-man digs out a bottle of bright blue pills from a corner cupboard and gives them to him. Says: 'These pills are highly dangerous and powerful, so only take one before you go out on this date. They'll make you feel randier than you'd ever imagined and for longer than you'd ever imagined.'

Uncle Angus is so carried away with his great expectation of the dickens of a good time, that he swallows the whole bottle.

Next morning he rings up the doctor. 'Can I have some liniment, please.'

Doctor laughs. 'Ho, ha, he, hi. Worked did they?'

'Yes,' says Uncle Angus.

'Right,' says the witch-doctor. 'I'll send along some liniment for your back.'

'Not my bleeding back. They got 'flu and didn't turn up. I need the liniment for my wrist.'

Meanwhile, back at Arturia Legend, yours very truly, Jonathan May has been considerably discomknockerated.

'Roger you rigid, Mrs. Legend?' I squawk, like a parrot trapped in its cage door by the long and featheries.

'Yes, please. And call me Artie.'

'But, but but.' More of these buts and I shall start feeling a bit of a goat. Uncle Nick had a mate on National Service who used to like a bit of a feel of a sheep. In the Navy he was, and he got caught with his wick in the sheep-dip.

At the court-martial, he tried two defences. First of all he said he thought it was a Wren in a duffle-coat. When that didn't work, he said it was foggy, and that he was having a pee in a field when a sheep backed on to him.

'Didn't they tell you at the clinic just what my little ... problem is?'

'No. Mar ... Miss Thrustinne merely said that you had a little ... problem, and that I would soon find out about it. And that I was to do what I could to help you.'

Arturia's eyes light up like she's a little girl who's been offered Donny Osmond's armpit to hang on the wall.

'Oh, I'm sure you'll be able to help me ever such a lot. I've had lots of psychiatrists. All shapes and sizes. None of them could cure me.'

'I was afreud of that,' I joke.

'Sorry?'

'Perhaps you were too jung for it.'

'Young?'

'Jung.'

There is a noise like frozen bathwater rumbling down a very long pipe that I am amazed to discover is the said lady laughing.

'Jung. Very funny indeed, Jonny. It is Jonny, isn't it? That's what they told me.'

'Yes. I'm little Jonny.'

'Little!!!!'

Had I belted her round the mush with a pair of wet Y-Fronts she couldn't have looked more shocked.

'Actually, Artie, not really little. But, modesty and all that. I'm sure you understand.'

She does.

Actually, I know very well what a lot of you suspicious folk are thinking. It's Old Jonny making it up to give himself (and us) a thrill. There aren't really ladies like this one.

Are there?

I can almost hear Tracy in Bought Ledgers panting while she waits for the answer. And even that nice young bloke who's just joined as a trainee rep – the one with the long hair – is panting in short breaths. Makes a change from breathing in short pants.

Well, I shall just tell you the whole dreadful tale of my afternoon in London with Mrs. Legend, and I shall leave it to you to decide for yourselves whether I'm kidding or not.

Actually, I don't believe her myself.

'Artie, I'm rather new at this ...'

'Oh. I prefer them with lots of experience.' When she says: 'lots', she licks her lips like a Heathrow cabbie when he sees five Japanese looking lost.

'No. I'm experienced at ... that ... but I'm new to this therapy.'

By now we are at the Tube Station and I have to buy us tickets to somewhere. Piccadilly Circus seems as good as anywhere for starters.

On the way down the escalators, Arturia tells me more about

her hang-up, and I begin to wonder how much of it is just in her mind. And how much of it is somewhere else.

'It's because of my second husband. The late Mister Legend.'

'Funny name,' I comment.

'Yes. When we got married his name was Herbert Shrunke-Wyllie. But I do draw the line at that, don't you?'

Don't answer that, folks.

'So shortly before he died, he changed it by deed-poll to Legend. Just liked the word, I suppose.'

'Sorry I never met him. I always wanted to meet someone who became a legend in their own lifetime.'

The Underground train is fairly crowded, but there are still quite a few seats left. To my surprise, Arturia ignores them and insists on standing squashed in a corner by the doors at one end of the train. Because of the noise, I find that I need to stand close to her to hear the rest of her case history. It is rather a potted history, but interesting.

No. I don't mean that Mrs. Legend is drunk. Potted means shortened. Like when a man goes into cold water. You could say he had a potted Edgar.

'Herbert was very repressed. And insisted on only having relations when all the doors were locked and the curtains pulled.'

'But how did his relations get in to see you if all the doors were locked?'

'Silly boy. I mean *this* sort of relations.'

I have a moment to wonder what the rest of the passengers must think. Here is this stunningly handsome man pressed in a corner by this prim lady. Probably a maiden aunt. With a smart hat on her maiden head. Not to mention Slough. And her clothes made in Hong Kong. (Maiden Hong Kong!)

What's good enough for Her Majesty . . .

(Publisher's Note: I hope that doesn't get us all thrown in the Tower.)

Oh, I don't know. Haven't been to Blackpool for years. Is

that bloke still there who used to come up through the floor in front of all the ladies playing this enormous organ?

Where was I before I was so rudely interrupted? On this train with a raving loonie!

I bet the other travellers are wondering why this above-mentioned handsome young man has suddenly gone as red as a beetroot and shot several feet up in the air. And why his dear old aunt is cuddling him in such a fond way. Perhaps he is shy of such public affection?

Perhaps.

And then again, perhaps Jonny May isn't used to having a respectable lady nearly old enough to be his mum grab him by the long and curlies on an Underground train between Bounds Green and Piccadilly. It's not as though we were going to Cockfosters.

Not only does she seize Edgar in a death grip that brings tears running down my leg, but she has also grabbed my hand and shoved it through a slit in the side of her skirt.

She smiles gently at me and whispers: 'Come on. Shoot me the juice, Jonny!' with an expression on her face that I'm sure makes everyone watching imagine that she is offering her pink-faced nephew a Rowntrees fruit gum.

'Not here!' I hiss, like an enraged cobra. Which is not a Japanese shoe-repairer.

'Yes. That's the point. Come on. Press up tight, lower yourself a bit and then straighten up.'

By sheer brute force she is dragging Edgar nearer the passion pit. Normally, I would be delighted to be so assaulted, or even a'peppered, but not just outside Caledonian Road Station.

Unlike many a good orange, I am saved by the crush. At Caledonian Road, a lot more people sweep aboard. The turnings-out from the afternoon Bingo session by the conversation. I pretend to be pushed away from Arturia, and manage to cover Edgar and my embarrassment with a copy of the 'E*e*i*g S*a*d*r*' that has been dropped on a seat.

She looks very disappointed at our separation, and I grin ruefully, shrugging my shoulders. Pretending it wasn't my fault. Like certain professional footballers when caught by the referee in some spectacularly nasty piece of calculated mayhem.

We finally descend at what my old mum always refers to as Piccalilli Circus. But then again she's always getting in a pickle!

One of the big troubles with my mum is that she's a dreadful hypochondriac. No, that doesn't mean she's nutty about stealing things from supermarkets. Hypochondria means someone who reckons they're constantly ill. Now I'm not saying that my old mum's really like that, but she's already ordered her tombstone and it says on it: 'There! I *told* you I was ill!'

I am so worried about Arturia's odd desires that I try and give her the impression that I'm walking with her, while I give the impression to everyone else that I'm not. She stares up at Eros, and I see her eyes light up at the idea of having it away up on the steps. Fortunately there are workmen hosing down the stones and the prospect is too chilling.

We stroll along Piccadilly while she tries to make up her mind where she wants to go. I slip into Hatchards book-shop to make sure they're still stocking my books. Good stocking-fillers my books. On the way back up after merry discourse with the manager of department, Arturia dives at my legs and I have to break through with the skill and grace of Gareth Edwards dodging a tackle.

Must ask that manager why he keeps on putting my books in the fiction section. Can't be right. That implies that they aren't all true. And we know better.

Don't we?

Don't we?!?!?

'Waxworks!' exclaims Mrs. Legend, leering at a passing policeman with such evil meaning that the poor man makes a grab for his truncheon. I am grateful that for a few minutes

Artie hasn't been making any grabs for mine. I don't like the idea of Edgar being up for grabs.

'Madame Tussauds?'

'Or even just one sword,' she suggests, digging me in the ribs. If I didn't know better I'd reckon she was on the booze. She resembles a Sunday School teacher less and less with every passing minute.

As Miss Thrustinne has given me ample of the folding stuff, I hail a taxi. I'd like to snow it, but the weather's too warm. Arturia climbs in the back, hitching up her skirt to show an amount of leg that makes Edgar turn in his groin.

There is the usual traffic jam as we plod along towards Baker Street and the famous waxworks. Crowds bustle by, several of them staring in the back of the cab with a more than passing interest. It is not until I glance sideways at my patient that I spot the reason.

'Pull your skirt down. You'll have us both arrested for indecent exposure.'

'Oooh, you say the nicest things, Jonny, darling. You know just what turns me on, don't you?'

Without more ado, and I'd rather there was more adon't, she is on top of me, one hand going for Edgar, the other pulling her black skirt up to grant me visiting rights to her tunnel of love.

'No. Not here! For the ... Aaaargh! Get your foot off my joystick! Please!'

'Come on, Jonny. I've not had it away in a taxi for over a week now.'

A week! By Clunk and Click! Why does she have this odd desire to do it in such public places? Why not just ordinary pubic places like other folk?

'Jonny. Come on. A cab's lovely. Hansom is as hansom does I always say.'

'Sick.'

'What?'

'Always feel sick in cars. And buses.' Think of return journey to the clinic. Add hastily: 'And tube trains. Sorry, Artie. Just leave me alone and don't even talk. I'll be all right. But if I think about making love, much as I'd like to, then it brings on motion sickness. And I don't want just to go through the motions.'

Mrs. Legend turns all motherly, which is about right considering her age. For once her mind is off thingie, although she insists on telling me about how hung-up her late husband was.

'I always say that it's a poor lover that blames his tool, don't you, love?'

'Yes.'

'Herbert used to take a bath with his clothes on so that he'd never have to catch sight of his little dangler. Not a mighty weapon like you've got in there, Jonny. He was so terrified of anyone catching us at it, that it made me want to do it whenever I could with as many people around as possible. Sort of shocking old Herbert, wherever the poor old sod's gone.'

'Gone?'

'Up? Or down? I just don't know.'

We rattle slowly along towards our destination, the meter clicking merrily away like a demented grasshopper. The fare is already so high that I wonder if it's some new scale that means you get to keep the taxi at the end of the journey.

'I'd have loved to have been a lady of the streets, you know. Done it actually on the pavements, with lines of men all queuing up for next go.'

Her hand has vanished beneath her skirt as she talks, so I imagine her underclothing has got in some disarray and she's straightening it. And any of you who can think up any other reason must have more imagination than me.

I try and get her mind off it by relating a related anecdote about one of my relations. The beautiful little sister who I have not fortunately seen for several months.

Melanie.

Though I do have an occasional card from her. The last one is posted in Casablanca. It says simply: 'Dear brother. Weather hot. Men lovely. Am constantly under the weather. Am also constantly under the men. Love from M.'

The anecdote concerns the time that poor Melanie is busted by the boys in blue, who allege that she has been on the game in Moseley. Or was it Edgbaston? The case comes up in court and the policeman alleges that she went to bed with a man.

'Yes. I did. I went to bed with him just because he was so nice.'

'But he gave you twenty pounds for it,' says the judge.

Melanie flashes her twin beams on him and simpers. 'Yes, my lord. Wasn't that a *nice* thing for him to do.'

Fortunately, Madame Tussauds isn't very crowded, which doesn't turn on my lovely companion. We flash (!) round the exhibits, which I must say I find a bit unsettling. I can't say it's my scene. I like scenes that can be heard as well as seen.

We amble along to the Chamber of Horrors, which I like a lot more. There is one particular character there who looks exactly like my Publisher. Since he is shown suffering an agonising fate, I cheer up. There is a wicked lady there who looks uncommonly like Melanie.

Don't get the idea that my brother and sister are all bad.

Well . . .

Melanie is keen on sports. Some sports. Though I remember the last time she played mini-golf. Everyone took the mickey.

The attendant there is talking to another, telling him that there is a large party of American tourists on their way round. I am holding Artie by the elbow, and I feel her quiver like someone's jammed five hundred volts up her Khyber.

'No.' I say.

At least it's dark.

I remember that Miss Thrustinne has told me to do my best

to keep the patients happy. I just wonder if she'll pay my fine.

I'm worried in case the heat we're generating might melt the exhibits. I'm sure that Crippen's nose is running. Well, just don't expect me to go running after it. Though I'd do anything to get out of this place. It's really creepy, though it's not putting Arturia off her stroke.

Nor is Edgar put off, and he is enjoying the stroking. My patient has taken charge, and I suss out that the quicker we get it over the quicker we can flee the scene. Or is it actually a tableau we're having it off in the middle of?

I used to enjoy playing patience, as well. Now I have the black queen firmly on top of my poor old red king. Torture through the ages is what it says on the sign, and it's torture I'm going through. I can hear the braying tones of the Americans as they go round the Chamber.

Maybe they won't see us in the dark.

'Will they see us in the dark?' whispers my little black widow. 'You know, I've never actually been caught at the very moment that I . . . you know . . . sort of finish. I do believe that if I could experience that just once that it might cure me of this.'

She may even get her wish. Jonny is getting ready to wind up the business of the meeting as fast as possible, but the tourists are getting closer with every second that passes. I am deeply involved with Artie, and I can feel certain muscles beginning to flutter like a landlady's heart as rent day comes around.

'Here we see various scenes of torture taking place in the gloom of a medieval dungeon,' intones the assistant to his onlookers.

'Let's have some light?' asks one of them, and I mutter a prayer to my guardian angel, who replies for once and we remain hidden in the darkness.

Artie is still moving. Slowly, but with very deep gripping, pinning me to the chair I'm sitting on. The combination of the tension and the movement, plus more suction than my old mum ever got out of her Hoover, is bringing me to the brink of the cliff.

Not Richard, you nit!

'Witness the horror on the face of the victim as he endures the agonising embrace of the Iron Maiden!'

'I'm coming, Jonny!' hisses Mrs. Legend, coming down so hard I almost expect to see Edgar appear out of the top of her head.

I can hear the Americans are becoming restless. The guide is so used to the tableau that he doesn't notice one of the waxworks is less wax and doing more work.

'It looks disgusting!' screeches one blue-rinse lady.

'I shall never come again!'

'Elmer! I'm going!'

'I'm coming, Evadne!'

'I'm coming, Artie.'

'Are you coming ladies and gentlemen?'

'I'm coming, Jonny!'

'I said I'm not coming again, and I mean that. I shall never come here again. I'm shocked.'

'Oh,' goes Mrs. Legend.

'Oh,' go the Americans.

'Oh,' I go.

I have never seen so much coming and going in my life.

It actually looks as though we might even get away with it in the darkness and confusion.

They should never have turned on the lights.

The worst thing is that the chair falls over and Edgar suffers a nasty case of splinters. There is a deal of unpleasant shouting, but we manage to slip out in the end. I have already slipped out of the end before the lights come on.

I call a cab. I can't remember what I call it, but things are still confused. Arturia is overwhelmed with delight at what has happened and claims she is miraculously cured. When I try to kiss her on the cheek by way of celebration, she slaps me on the face.

'Really, Jonny. Not in the back of a taxi. Anyone might see us.'

I wonder if the clinic'll double my wages for a cure like that. And that's only the beginning.

CHAPTER FIVE

Edgar responds to a good wash and a careful going-over with a pair of tweezers. Which is just as well as there isn't anyone in this place actually qualified as a doctor.

But anything's better than some of the hospitals back home in Birmingham. I know one bloke who went in and asked this Brummie doctor there if he could be sterilised.

So they boiled him for thirty minutes!

I'm not sure whether Marilyn is pleased with what happens or not. I tell her about the cure, and she looks about as believing as that bloke on 'Mastermind' when someone gives a wrong answer.

'Mrs. Legend was going to pay us one hundred and fifty pounds a week for a three week stay here. She would have attended group therapy.'

'I reckon my grope therapy did her more good.'

'Possibly. She claims it has made her quite well, and stopped her desires to engage in sexual relations in public and exposed situations.'

'It's me who gets exposed. All she has to do is drop her skirt. Do my zip up too fast and I shall be there with the boy sopranos for the rest of my life.'

'I prefer to look on the bright side, Jonny. Through her psychiatric contacts she may well bring us other patients on her messages of our miracle treatment.'

I give her my broadest smile, which some ladies say makes me look like Robert Redford. Others say Great-Uncle Bulgaria, but they are mainly the jealous.

'On the other hand ...' here comes that cold front again, bringing another damned deep depression. 'On the other hand you have lost us nearly five hundred pounds. Have you got anything to say?'

'I'll pay for any damage,' I try, putting on my best Michael Crawford impersonation. It goes down like a wedding ring on a Cardinal.

'Jonny. It is late. We've all had a trying day. I suggest we all go to bed.'

'Well, Marilyn. I'm not sure I'm up to much after all that happened this afternoon.'

'Jonny. You will go to your bed and I will go to mine. Goodnight!'

Am I to be ordered around like that?

Is Jonny a man or a mouse?

Can she dismiss me to a lonely bed, just like some servant?

I shall stand up and say just what I want.

'Goodnight Marilyn.'

Tomorrow is the first day of the rest of your life.

Two rousing cheers.

I sleep badly in a vast bed that looks like it was made for a retired elephant. My old man once had a rotten job one summer. There were a lot of travelling circuses up round the Midlands and he had to follow the elephants.

He reckoned he could have cleaned up!

Worst part was trying to get three pregnant elephants into a railway wagon. When the old man had downed a few pints of cooking he used to get mixed up and claim his job was getting three elephants pregnant in a railway wagon!

But the sun is shining like it's come unglued from a packet of Corn Flakes. I love those breakfast ads. 'I have two men in my life – and my case comes up next week.'

Breakfast at the clinic is a long way off what my old mum serves up back home in Brum. For instance, the bacon looks like bacon, not like something that's fallen off the bottom of an old car. And the eggs at the clinic would fail if one tried to use them to patch up a hole in the guttering. And the porridge . . . !

We once have a bloke round from the council who offers my mum a contract for supplying them with her porridge to botch up the holes in M5 and M6. Unfortunately on that particular day we have scrambled eggs. Looks like the porridge, but lacks that charred roughness.

Marilyn doesn't appear for breakfast, nor do any of the other staff at the clinic. In fact, I am not all that sure there are any more staff around. There's Miss Tanner in the office. The Incredible Hulkess on the gate. Someone's cooked the meals, and I suppose there must be cleaners. But no nurses. And no serious-looking men in white coats running around with clip-joints. Sorry. Clip-boards.

After the meal, I wander about the grounds with my coffee. I could call them coffee grounds but that might be grounds for you shutting the book. So, I'm not going to say it. My old mum's coffee has sometimes been mistaken for vegetable soup by those not in the know.

My Uncle Nick once opens a restaurant in Birmingham. First item on the menu is 'Soup In A Basket.'

I finally get a summons to appear before Miss Thrustinne at eleven. I brush my brush-denim shirt so that I look my usual immaculate self and comb back my forelock.

Fore-LOCK! Missus! It's what you tug. The bit that hangs down at the front. The bit that gets greasy and you have to keep pushing it back.

I give up.

The oak door of Room Sixty-nine is still in the pink as I brush it gently with my knuckles.

'Come in, Jonny.'

Music to my ears. This time my hand has no trouble with the knob. Those knobs are rotten when they're sticky, aren't they ladies? Marilyn is sitting on her desk, talking to someone on the phone. She smiles at me, which means I haven't got the order of the boot yet, and waves me to a chair.

I sit down, and twiddle my thumbs, watching my boss in dynamic action. She's a real action girl. Bendable joints and special gripping hands. But unlike Action Girl, Marilyn has some really interesting accessories to interest men.

She crosses her legs and I see that she is still not wearing any . . . wait for it . . . tights!

Boo and Hiss! Sorry to disappoint you, but she *is* wearing . . . here it comes . . . knickers! Not that they are very heavy duty material. As pussy-pelmets go, they are scarcely draught-proof. They are more transparent than the average gold-fish bowl. Incidentally, my sister Melanie used to think that a goldfish bowl was a pregnant jamjar.

'That's good . . . That's good . . . That's bad . . . That's good . . . That's good . . .'

What can she be doing? Who can she be talking to on the phone? I wonder if she can be grading eggs.

'That's very good . . . Rather bad . . . That's good . . . That's excellent . . .'

Eggshellent?

No, I'm only yolking! I'm afried so. And I'm rather hard-boiled, you know. I won't poach any other jokes about eggs for the rest of the book.

(Publisher's Note: I wish that I could believe Mister May's promises.)

They're more reliable than some people. He promised to buy his wife a new house with a rural outlook. If you can call Harrow sewerage works rural? That's why he always looks so flushed. He's clean round the bend.

At last Miss Thrustinne is finished on the phone and receives the replacer. Gives me another smile.

'Hello, Jonny. That's our next patient ringing to say she'll be here before lunch, so I'll hand her over to you for the afternoon's treatment. And please try not to cure her too quickly. I want word to get about that we're good but not that good.'

'I shall do my best, Marilyn. I mean, I shall not do my best to do my worst. What's wrong with this lady? Not another one who wants to do it on top of Nelson's Column?'

'No. Quite the reverse. Miss Tite-Quyne has a very different problem.'

With a name like that the mind boggles at what it can be. As long as it's not doing it in the street and frightening the horses, I'm not too worried. I can handle most things.

'Perhaps I ought to tell you, Jonny. Specially after what happened last time when I didn't tell you.'

'I am a gog.' I don't know what that means. You never hear about anyone actually being *the* gog, do you?

'Well. Hernia Tite-Quyne has ...'

'Hernia!!!'

'Yes, Jonny. That is her name!'

Icicles drop from Miss Thrustinne's lips, but I cannot stop myself.

'I hope she'll truss me to help her. I mean. I shall give her my support and I hope she'll wear it constantly. I'd hate to have our relationship ruptured by ...'

'Jonny!'

By Fawlty and Towers! That had the real whipcrack note to it. I shut up and look attentive.

'Better. Hernia is coming to spend a little time with us because she suffers from an incapacity to reach climatic satisfaction.'

'You mean she can't come?'

'I wish you wouldn't put it so crudely, but that is correct.'

I wish I could put it anyhow.

'Not at all?'

'Not at all.'

'Not ever?'

'Not ever.'

My heart bleeds for this poor little church-mouse of a lady. I vow to do my best for her. I shall lay on a supreme exhibtion of my skill. Within minutes I shall have her biting the carpet and begging for more.

'Jonny?'

'Yes.'

'If you had a large illuminated notice across your forehead, it would not be easier to read your thoughts. You are thinking in that nasty little chauvinist mind that you are God's gift to women, and that this poor woman will spend five minutes in your bed and then be rolling on the floor in a frothing passion of lust begging you for more. Aren't you?'

'Errr, well, but, sort of, like, errr, ummm that is to say I . . .'

She shakes her head like the Chancellor confronted with yet another lame duck. 'It will not be like that Jonny. And I would urge you to remember the wise words on the subject. There is no such thing as a frigid woman. Only clumsy and selfish men.'

You can't top that, can you? I guess there is something in that saying. But, then again, there's a great truth in most famous sayings.

Like the one that decorates the walls of some of the better establishments of the land. The first person complains:

'This bleeding crapper is no use at all,
The seat is too high and the hole is too small.'

Beneath it, in another hand, is the immortal reply:

'To that I must tender the obvious retort:
Your ass is too big and your legs are too short!'

I sit staring at a lovely bit of breast all through lunch, but nobody offers me second helpings of the chicken, so I have an extra-large chunk of spotted dog to make up. I'm still a growing lad.

Miss Tite-Quyne doesn't appear, and Marilyn tells me that the lady is shy. I'm not surprised. I wouldn't fancy going in to some strange bird and admitting that I couldn't get it up. There's only one thing worse than being all dressed up and nowhere to go. It's being undressed and unable to come.

'She's in the Relaxation Suite, Jonny,' says Marilyn after lunch.

'The Suite's for the sweet, Eh?'

'Either control your tongue, or you may be looking for another vacancy.'

The thought of my tongue probing for a vacancy sets Edgar off in the right frame of mind for the afternoon's task. The Relaxation Suite is in the basement. I have been shown it on my lightning tour of the premises the previous day.

Someone has spent a load of bread on this place. The Relaxation Suite isn't all that big, but what there is down in the bargain basement is good.

Walls lined in imitation fur, and concealed lights round the corners of the room. Mirrors everywhere. Not that I personally dig that sort of scene. Mirrors. But on reflection ...

The bed is big enough for half a dozen coupling couples, and round. A white bedspread that's all soft and fluffy. There are some quad speakers around the place, and music drifting around. Not my idea of music to thingie by. Great Western themes. Not the railway! 'The Fat, The Thin And The Funny,' and 'The Return Of The Second Sons Of The Magnificent Seven Riding Again.'

There's nobody there so I pour myself a small shot from a very well-equipped bar. It would be my old man's idea of heaven. To lie on that bed, with naked birds pouring him large glasses of best bitter while he receives, consecutively, news of a West Bromwich Albion win at home and a West Bromwich victory away.

The Southern Comfort slips down with all the ease of a bankrupt in Fort Knox, and I am about to embark on a second and maybe a third when the door opens.

'Miss Tite-Quyne?'

Can't be. Must be a mistake. From what Marilyn tells me, I guess she'll be rather like poor Arturia, only much more so. I kind of imagine she's going to be a rather younger version of the late Queen Mary. All ice outside, but all ice inside as well.

'Hello. You're Jonny?'

'I'm May.'

'Yes. But I won't.'

She is not all that tall. Not all that skinny. Not exactly what you'd call fat. Just *very* well rounded. She has erogenous zones in places where other ladies just have places. She wears a pink negligée slit to the waist.

You're probably waiting to hear about the other clothes she's got on.

Keep waiting.

There aren't any.

A pink negligée, slit to the waist. And very obviously nothing else at all.

'They didn't tell me. Do you charge, Jonny?'

'No. No, I approach very slowly.'

She laughs. A slow, sexy laugh, and comes towards me, leaving her clothe behind her. Clothe? I don't see why that shouldn't be the word. And all of you lot of intellectuals who know that I'm wrong can take the information and write it on a long strip of paper. Roll it up into a tube, and . . .

Stuff it!

'Shall we lie down and make ourselves comfortable, Jonny? I'm told it's easier that way.'

'You've been told right, lady. You hop into bed and I'll peel off. Do you want the lights left on or not?'

'I don't mind. But I think I'd like to see what it is you've got to offer.'

She sounds like a rich lady shopping around for a best buy in electrical goods. Maybe there's a 'Which' report on the best thingie around. Tests for durability, length, finish, duration, ingenuity. I reckon that the May Edgar would come on top. Or underneath. I'm not proud.

And it's British, folks.

My clothes vanish into the thick carpet with hardly a ripple, and I join Hernia in between the satin sheets. I've sat in blankets and I've sat in chairs, but I've never satin sheets.

Thinking of which reminds me of a little jest. This Mexican

stays at this expensive Birmingham hotel. After a couple of days the chambermaid comes in to see if he needs anything.

'Everyting ees very good, sank you. I enjoy seeting watching television. Ees very good.'

'The bed all right, sir?'

'Sank you.'

'Would you like another sheet, sir?'

'No, sank you. I had three sheets already. Must be the English food!'

Well, I did say it was only a little jest.

Hernia is warm and very cuddly. I somehow expected that she'd be actually cold to touch, but she isn't. I devote a few minutes to my usual tongue exercises, kissing her on the lips and cheeks and eyes and neck and lower. Normally that brings the cherries up like miniature mountains, but it is ominous that nothing seems to be happening in that area. They remain as flat as one of my mum's soufflés.

She kisses away like any other lady with whom I've had the pleasure, and Edgar is given a twice-over. My ten burglars are giving of their best, risking a charge of assault with ten friendly weapons. It's difficult to describe what is happening without descending to rude words, but it's more a question of what isn't happening.

Everything.

How can I put it?

I didn't say *where* can I put it?

Look at it like this: If you have an ideal sponge-cake it should be moist and slightly sticky to the touch. And if there's something not right with the sponge-cake, then you probably find that it's all dry and crumbly to the touch.

Well, that's what's happening. I mean that's what isn't happening. Hernia's sponge-cake is not getting at all moist. I even cheat a bit and try to help out by licking it into shape, but I have seen more response from a marble tombstone. This is obviously not going to be as easy as I thought.

For the next ten minutes I do everything I can think of, and some I'd rather not think about.

Nothing.

Zero.

Zilch, as Kojak might say. Not even he could do anything, even if he went at it bald-headed.

'It's no good, Jonny. I'll never be able to come. Never. I shall never come again.'

My first instinct, like everyone else's in that sort of situation, is to be very sympathetic, but it suddenly strikes me that her tearful moans are just like Evel Knievel after he falls on his ass over a load of buses at Wembley. All that 'never, ever jump again.'

Few months later there he is at it again.

The thought of her being at it again in a few months after failing to come over a row of buses amuses me and I start to giggle. Hernia stops crying and pokes me with her forefinger. I'm still ahead because I've been poking her with ten fingers.

'You don't care. And I don't like that crazy music.'

'Bet you don't like rockin' bands either,' say I, the good old rock 'n roll lyrics getting me going into another fit of sniggering, but I still manage to get up and turn the sounds right off.

'I've heard of music while you jerk, but that's just ridiculous.'

'Jonny?' At least the tears have stopped, and she is lying still on her back.

'What?'

'Don't you think it's sad?'

I suppose it is, but I sort of guess that once I start giving her sympathy, then we shall have to go back to square one. 'Yes. In a way, but in another way it's rather funny. I was just thinking about how Evel Knievel keeps trying all these maniac jumps, and crashing. Just like you keeping trying to break through the sex barrier.'

'But he keeps failing, and so do I.'

'Yes, but you don't have to do it on a motor-bike like he

does. Anyway, he sometimes manages it, and everyone cheers him.'

While I'm talking, I have sent my ten commandoes on an underground diversionary movement. Surprise, surprise! That rather arid desert around the grope grotto is slowly becoming fertile.

Somehow, by not taking her too seriously, I reckon I've rumbled it. Poor old Hernia must have had a few bum lovers (and I mean bum as in bad and not as in anything that might send Sphere's lawyers scurrying for their blue pencils) at the beginning and didn't make it out of the pits. Or out of the paddock if you prefer a horsey expression.

Then she must have got a Tite-Quyne tightness every time and never looked back. When I glance across at her, I am pleased to see her face assuming that expression of sort of simpering idiocy that some ladies get when they're well on the way down the fairway. (Change to golf there).

Cautiously, as she has her eyes closed, I ease Edgar nearer what is rapidly turning from desert to paddy field. No, that isn't an Irish meadow! I sometimes wonder why I bother.

'Oh, Jonny. What's happening?'

'You're just beginning to feel the earth moving beneath you,' I say, kissing her hurriedly on the lips and rolling over into a good submission hold.

'Oooh!'

That's Edgar putting one in the back of the net. (Football now).

The ice is melting, and things are really beginning to hammer along, when I feel a certain stiffening. And I don't mean Edgar who has been all right for several minutes. I am talking about Hernia.

'Jonny?'

'Mmmm?' I don't like talking with my mouth full.

'It won't be any good. I just know it won't be any good . . .'

I muffle that still small voice of doubt by shoving my tongue into it. Then removing it.

'Hernia. Do you know what they call an uncircumcised Jewish child?'

'No?'

'A girl.'

It works again. I can feel that she's laughing again, and that takes her mind off her frigidity and rigidity. It's like being swallowed by an anaconda with hiccoughs, but more pleasant.

After that it's all downhill and she bucks and rears like the best of them, screaming at the top of her voice. The desert is absolutely flooded, and I wonder whether I ought to declare a state of emergency. But I am more concerned with hanging on both to her and the bed so that I can finish my own game.

I've hardly stopped the heavy breathing when she's after it again. This time we end up rolling around on the floor with her chewing the carpet.

I am aware that this going to cost the clinic another few hundred pounds, but I recall the immortal words of Bob Dylan. At last I see what he means. There's no success like failure, and failure's no success at all.

At least, I think I see what he means!

After Miss Tite-Quyne has packed her bags and gone away again, to practise what she's learned, I am summoned once again to the presence of Miss Thrustinne.

'Jonny May. Have you been sent here by some enemy of mine to wreck all my plans?'

'No.'

'Do you have to work so hard at being a damned idiot?'

'Just comes naturally. Anyway. Two miracle cures in two days. You can't complain.'

'I can't afford that sort of record. Any more cures and we're ruined.' See what Dylan means?

'I'm sorry.' I put on my little-boy lost face that either softens ladies' hearts or in the case of Liz James makes her turn away and simulate puking noises.

Marilyn falls for it, and smiles, reaching over the desk to pat my hand. 'No. It's me who should be sorry. When we feel ready to risk the media, I shall make sure you get the praise you deserve. You're a born therapist.'

'Next case, please, nurse,' I chirp.

'Aaah, well. Not just yet, darling. I think we'd better try something a little different for a day or two, so that our bank balance can recover.'

'What? I hope it's not stoking the boiler. I much prefer stoking ladies.'

'I have a friend who teaches human biology to girls at a finishing school. I think you might give her a hand for a lesson.'

'Help her with the birds and the bees, sort of thing?'

Marilyn puts her head on one side in a rather odd way. 'Yes. Jonny. That *sort* of thing.'

What can she mean?

CHAPTER SIX

So *that's* what she means!

By Fur, Till, Eyes and Asian! (Think about it!) But biology lessons have come on since my day. You were lucky then to get a quick glance at a rabbit's rumpo.

But now . . .

So many people know absolutely nothing about any of the facts of life, until they suddenly find they've got children and then they wonder how.

I remember going once to a maternity hospital with a mate whose wife was about to drop it. He wasn't too worried. But there was a bloke in the waiting-room who was like a cartoon character. Bitten finger-nails and ankle-deep in half-smoked cigarettes. There's another father-to-be there as well, but he tells us he's had eight already, so he's being very cool about it.

The nervous bloke keeps talking about having babies, and what's going to happen, and this experienced man keeps on reassuring him. The nervous one suddenly says: 'Here. Pardon me for asking, but I wonder how long it will be before I'm able to . . . you know . . . have intercourse with my wife after she's had the baby?'

The other bloke shakes his head. 'Can't really tell you that mate. Depends on whether she's in a private room or a public ward.'

Before giving you the dreadful details of what happens in the biology class, with all those young girls, I'd better give you an idea of the rest of the day. Don't think that working as a therapist in the clinic is all easy work.

In fact, I'm so knackered after the last couple of days that I spend most of the morning in bed. But I do manage to rise before lunch. Actually, I've risen long before then, but I go for a quick Jimmy and it goes away again.

Lunch is delicious. I ask for second helpings of the beef and Marilyn serves me herself, saying to my bewilderment: 'Must keep your strength up ready for this afternoon.'

Funny that.

I don't reckon you need a lot of strength to help a lady give a talk. Probably carry in her animals or assist with the slides. Not to mention the roundabouts!

I should have known. It's not that my guardian angel is bad. Just sloppy.

The lady running the class is called Anthea Didne-Dowel. I can only suppose that she is a fan of Bruce Forsyth.

'My gels will be coming soon,' she says, as an opening gambit. I can't think of any reply that won't either get my face slapped or lose me my job.

Miss Didne-Dowel is in her early fifties with a figure that would make an airship designer envious. I'm not saying that she's fat but Speak-Your-Weight machines simply beg her for mercy when she tries them. Iron grey hair pulled back in a tight little bun. Sensible tweed skirt. Twin-set in a sort of dirty-grey. And that's only her teeth. I don't want to give the impression that she wears big shoes, but if the canals ever make a come-back she could make a lot of money leasing them out to coal-hauliers.

'I'm terribly grateful to you for volunteering like this, Mister May. I'm sure that what you're doing will stand out for the gels and live long in their memories.'

I get a cold feeling at the base of my spine, rather like the time that Morrie puts two and a half pounds of maggots in the fridge and then tips them down my back while I'm watching 'Sale Of The Century.'

'Stand out.' 'Live long.' Those are phrases that I might

apply to a certain part of my anatomy. Five letters beginning with 'E'.

'Er . . . Just what exactly did Miss Thrustinne say that I would be doing to help you?'

There is a sound like an unoiled dungeon door scraping open. Since it comes from a large hole roughly in the middle of the biology teacher's face, I assume that it is what passes for a laugh in Miss Didne-Dowel's circles. And I bet they're ever-increasing circles.

'You're a gay blade, Mister May, and no mistake.' She gives me a nudge in the ribs that would unsettle Mick McManus. 'Pretending to a gel that you don't know. I do hope you aren't going to turn nervous on me?'

I notice that Marilyn has crept up behind me. 'Yes, Jonny. After all that's happened in the last couple of days, I too hope that you aren't thinking of backing out of your obligations.'

'Backing out!' I have bent over backwards to oblige in the past, with the exception of Rupert Colt, who was a very 'gay' blade indeed.

'I'm sure he won't, Anthea.' She smiles at me with lips thinner than Twiggy on a diet. 'After all, his wages won't be due for several days yet.' And she laughs like it's a joke, but I know better.

'Very well, Mister May. I suggest we get down to the lecture room and get ready for the gels.'

'Anything you say, Miss Didne-Dowel. But could I just ask you what . . .?'

Too late. She vanishes down the corridor faster than my old man when the landlord calls 'Time'. Marilyn gives me a pat on the bottom to speed me on my way.

I turn to her. 'Marilyn? Couldn't you just give me a clue?'

'Yes. Of course. 'Rapid growth within the Perineum, perhaps. Twelve letters.'

It is clear that I am going to get sweet nothing doings out of her, so I slump along the passage after the shrinking figure of the biology teacher. Miss Thrustinne calls after me: 'Jonny. If you want a serious clue . . .?'

'I do.'

'Well. Perhaps if I give you some advice.'

'What?'

'If the worst comes to the worst, then I suggest you try to grin and bear it.'

'Bear it'? What can she mean by that? Is it going to be something hard that I have to bear? Something long I have to bear?

The answer to both of those questions might be 'Yes'. But the word is not 'bear'. It is 'bare'!

There are about twenty girls in Miss Didne-Dowel's class. I guess their average age is about eighteen, with a couple of them looking more like a well-preserved thirty. Seeing that row of bright innocent faces, masking minds, no doubt, of utter depravity, reminds me of the horrors that dogged me when I was a games master at a similar school. They dogged me, until I was cowed. I shouted 'til I was hoarse.

But those of you are loyal fans (both of you) will already have read about this in 'Confessions Of A Games Master', published by Sphere Books and available from all good bookshops and most good newsagents. Those of you who haven't yet read every word of all of my rib-ticklers had better go straight out and get them now. Unless it's the middle of the night. I don't want hordes of you going around knocking-up booksellers. If there's any knocking-up to be done, then I'm the one.

There are more leers than at the Royal Shakespeare Theatre and more winks than in a tiddly competition. And more suggestions than a conference of Young Liberals. It is clear that Miss Anthea hasn't got a strong hold on the girls. Looking around at some of them, I wouldn't mind having a go at coming to grips with them.

'Drop them; come on!'

'Get them down!'

'Show us your ding-a-ling!'

There are also wolf-whistles!

By Fem and Lib but this is a bit much! I am not used to young ladies behaving like this. I believe that a woman's place is in the home, washing and cooking and all that. Just like a mistress is something that comes between a mattress and her master. Still, I suppose this is a trend up with which we shall all have to put.

But the first girl who pinches my bottom will get a belt round the mush. Just like I've got in my time. If it's equality they want, then it's equality they can have.

'Gels! Gels!'

She has as much effect on her crew as a fart in a thunderstorm. I stand there smiling sheepishly as they carry on playing the goat. I must stop these farmyard figures of speech!

'Please! Gels. Can I have a little silence for Mister May?'

At last the noise level sinks fractionally below that of Concorde passing by twenty miles away, which means it's just possible to hear yourself think. Miss Didne-Dowel makes a gesture to me. At first I think she is telling me to go away and my hopes rise.

Nothing else does.

Then I realise she is simply indicating that I should sit down. There is still this grim feeling of foreboding. Or even fiveboding. I shake myself to try and get rid of this stupid fear. Really! This is a perfectly respectable lady with a class of . . . junior sex maniacs . . . in a perfectly . . . secret sex clinic.

Gulp!

I am becoming putrified with fear. Or should that be petrified? I never was any good with words. Watch out for the bit of snidery from my Publisher!

(Publisher's Note: As Mister May attended neither a good public school nor a university as I did, I am hardly surprised he has trouble with words.)

Yeah, smartiepants, but I don't have any trouble with birds. And my school wasn't that bad. At least it was approved!

Thinking about getting mixed up with words reminds me of what happens to a mate of my old man back home in Brum.

His name is Fat Freddy Wells.

Not my old man!

Fat Freddy's name is Fat Freddy Wells.

Get it? Got it? Good.

Fat Freddy goes to this local hospital and asks to see a surgeon. Tells him that he wants to be castrated.

'What?' boggles the medic, wondering if his hearing-aid is packing up on him.

'I want to be castrated,' repeats Fat Freddy.

'You realise that the operation you want is connected with your sexual organ?'

'Yeah. Trim my chopper. I come in to be castrated and that's what I want.'

'Well. We have a vacant bed,' (This might make you think it's not a true story but miracles do happen. Even in National Health hospitals in Birmingham!)

So, despite all their attempts to change his mind from taking this drastic step, Fat Freddy is absolutely determined about being castrated.

They perform the operation that afternoon, and Fat Freddy comes round from the anost . . . anetsht . . . anaesthiat . . . gas. Finds his lamb lunger gift-wrapped in yards of bandages and three doctors standing round the bed watching him.

'Mister Wells?' says one of them.

'Yeah,' says F.F.

'I don't know how to say this. Perhaps if I am a little circumspect . . .'

And Fat Freddy begins to cry. '*That* was the word. Oh Gawd! *That* was the word!

Miss Didne-Dowel ignores the naughty comments from her

young charges. Personally, I'd rather there was no charge at all. Certainly not from this bright brigade.

'Today I am going to offer you a new and very exciting experience. Mister May is going to assist me with a lecture on the human reproductive system.'

That iced water is flowing freely down my back again. She can't be going to say . . .

'Thanks to my good friend, Marilyn Thrustinne, we are able to use the facilities of her new clinic. And I must repeat that I do not want anything that happens here this afternoon to leak out.'

If I have my way there won't be anything *to* leak out. Then I spot that there is a sort of spectators' gallery over the room, and that my boss is standing there with what I think writers call an enigmatic smile playing round her lips. Much as I'd like to play round her lips, I get the message. I don't know what she does to her patients, but by the Bull and the Ring she terrifies me.

For the next minute she talks at a fast lick (!) about what I suspect is how you do thingie and what happens after you've done thingie. But she uses words that I've never heard of. Makes it sound more like a cookery lecture with all her chat about how the eggs aren't ready yet.

She also goes on a lot about: 'The brave little army battles on upstream, through all manner of hostile forces, gradually becoming fewer and fewer until one last lone survivor reaches his goal.'

Sounds like John Wayne in the 'Alamo' to me.

The girls all take notes, and I guess that they are actually a bit frightened of Miss Didne-Dowel. Maybe they have an exam to pass.

One of the young ladies in the front row waits until the teacher has turned away to write something on the board, and then holds up something for me to see. The light is reflected off the paper and I have to squint.

Looks like a sort of candle.

Or a marrow.

Or is it a . . .?

It is.

'We saw last week how the urino-genital apparatus of the rabbit was constructed.'

She ought to go and wash out her mouth using all these dirty words in front of girls young enough to be my lovers. I mean her daughters.

'Now, we shall move from the rabbit to Mister May.'

What?

'And we shall see that there is a great similarity between them.'

What, what! ! !

She turns to me with what passes for a welcoming smile. I try to smile but find that someone has snuck up on me and poured quick-setting concrete into my face muscles.

'Right, Mister May. Would you like to come up here with me?'

Frankly, there is absolutely nothing at all further from my thoughts at that moment.

'Come now. Don't be shy.'

'Maybe he had it blown off in the war,' comments a dewy-eyed angel in the second row. I am more frightened by that second row than I would have been by Willy-John McBride.

Miss Didne-Dowel ignores it and comes across and leads me up on the stage by the hand. I am shaking more than the first time I see Tina Turner live.

'We're ready.'

I'm not.

Out of the corner of my eye I see Marilyn and she is pretending to fire a gun at me. I get the picture. Yes, I see.

With an infinite slowness, I start to take down my trousers. Wondering when was the last time that Bounds Green was devastated by an earthquake.

'Please be a little quicker, Mister May. There's only half an hour of the lesson left.'

I speed up to something like approximating to a badly-ruptured tortoise. Things are not helped by the girls starting a low chant of: 'Off! Off!! Off!!!'

In what seems to me like three and a quarter seconds, I am down to my trousers. A pretty girl in the front row – the one who did the naughty drawing – keeps licking her lips in a way that I would normally find a turn-on. But not now.

I have goose-pimples on top of my goose-pimples. The eyes of the world seem to be watching me. I suss out that Edgar is also extremely upset. What worries me most is that he will vanish altogether.

'And the trousers, please Mister May!'

There is a sharp note in Miss Didne-Dowel's voice, and the howling of the mob is turning nasty.

I get a chilling draught playing round my pawnbrokers. And no I haven't got three of them. In future I shall have more sympathy for those poor Christians who get fed to the lions.

'And the underpants, Mister May.'

I hope they're grateful for what they are about to get a butchers at. Even the Labour might be better than this dreadful experience. A bank manager considering an application for an overdraft moves faster than me. And with a lot more enthusiasm as well.

But at last it's done. There I stand, nakeder than nature intended. At least Edgar hasn't totally vanished, but I wouldn't reckon my chances in getting a centrefold job in a ladies' magazine. If there are any dykes around with holes in them that need stopping, then just don't call on Edgar.

Not that sort of dyke! Dutch ones.

'Excellent.'

That's Anthea, adjusting her glasses on the end of her nose as though they've got a bit steamed-up. In fact, I reckon that Anthea's getting a bit steamed-up herself at actually having the real thing instead of a boring drawing in a text-book. I'm relieved that Edgar isn't in the shape to do any boring. That would be good for my ego, but too embarrassing to even think about.

Fortunately, I don't see any chance of it happening. I'm not averse (like some poets) to ladies past their first flush of youth. I used to go out with an attendant from a ladies' loo and she was well past the first flush. But Anthea isn't my type. I don't even mind joining in naughtiness with anyone who isn't too skinny. But Miss Didne-Dowel makes Cyril Smith look like David Hemery.

'There. Now you gels can actually see what we've been talking about. Those are the male genitals. Now you can see the strong resemblance to a rabbit.'

After a bit, I actually don't find it as awful as I thought I would. The girls are all busy taking notes as Miss Didne-Dowel rabbits on about rabbits. Edgar ignores all the chat, and I find that I can stare at the ceiling and pretend that all this isn't happening. If my old mum could see me now, she'd throw a fit. Plus plates and knives and cups.

I remember there's once a dreadful row when this divorced lady moves in next door to us. Quite a pretty lady. My old man isn't that hot at hiding his feelings, and mum gets a bit peed off about the way Mrs. Bumsore is always slipping in to borrow something. She reckons that it's dad that Mrs. Bumsore really wants to borrow.

Incidentally, it is her ex-husband who wrote that famous book: 'Riding For Beginners.' By Major Bumsore!

Anyway, everything comes to a head between my old mum and Mrs. Bumsore one afternoon when mum's out at the shops and my old man's getting ready to go out. But, let him tell the story himself.

'I was goin' to the bleedin' dogs and my trousers had got two bleedin' buttons missin' off the bleedin' flies. Mrs. Bumsore comes round to borrow a cup of sugar and sees me strugglin' with the bleedin' needle. Offers to sew them on for me. Well, I wasn't goin' to bleedin' refuse, am I?'

No, he's not. If he had it would have ruined the story.

'I'm in a hurry, so I don't take them off. She just kneels

down and sews them on for me, neat as a bleedin' whistle. So far, so bleedin' good. The trouble comes when she has to cut off the loose ends of bleedin' cotton. Can't find any scissors. So there I am, standin' in our bleedin' parlour with my flies open, and Mrs. Bumsore on her hands and knees in front of me. As she can't find the bleedin' scissors, she decides she'll have to bite off the loose ends of the bleedin' thread with her teeth. And, it's at *that* very moment that mum comes back from her shoppin'!!'

There's only five minutes to go when disaster rears its head.

And that's not all that rears.

'I think all we need to do now gels is complete our sketches.'

'Please, Miss Didne-Dowel?'

'Yes Petulia?'

It's the little darling from the front row, who smiles at me while she talks to Miss Anthea. 'The light isn't very good to draw by. The model's genitalia are in a pool of darkness. Truly.'

'Yes. Yes, I see what you mean. Or rather I don't see.' There is **that** frightful noise again that indicates the lady thinks she has made a joke.

I glance down at Edgar who seems perfectly obvious to me, and not at all hidden in the shadows. But if they want me to move a bit... The idea of showing off in front of these ladies is beginning to get rather fun.

Until...

'Perhaps if I held it.'

'No!'

'Please keep quiet, Mister May.'

'If I went and stood by him, I could sort of hold it out in my hand so that we could all get to see it a lot better.'

The very idea! Having this slip of a girl coming out and holding my pork chopper between her... Down Edgar! Between her fingers so that I'd be able to feel... Down Edgar!!

'I don't think that's really a good idea, Petulia! I'm sure

you have the best of motives for making the suggestion,' (I don't), 'but if anyone is to hold the genitalia I think it had better be me.'

There is a gleam in her eye like Margaret Thatcher watching Ted Heath sink slowly in the west. All the girls are looking at her, smothering their giggles in hands and in handkerchiefs. None of them has yet noticed the dreadful effect that the idea is having on Edgar. The more I try not to think about 'it', the more 'it' goes on. And on.

'But if I could sort of pull it out and . . .'

That does it.

'Oooooooooh!'

'Miss!!'

'Look!!'

'Mister May !!!!'

'I'm sorry, but . . .'

I try to apologise for the way that Edgar has . . . exceeded his authority. I don't want to put it more crudely, but I think it stands out a mile. I mean . . . you know.

The girls are all jumping up on their chairs screaming like they've seen a mouse. But I'm not a mouse, so maybe they just want a better look.

Miss Didne-Dowel is looking like the Mummy has just risen from its tomb. Like a museum curator whose exhibits have started coming to life. Which in a way I suppose they have. Or it has.

Trying to ignore Edgar's elevation, I take a step towards the biology teacher, in an attempt to reassure her that if nothing else, my intentions remain honourable. It is a vain attempt.

She looks at me like I'm the Blagdon amateur rapist, and screams at the top of her voice. I take another step forward but it is no good.

'I'll get it out of this mess.' That's what I intend to say.

'I've got it out and I'll put it up your dress,' is what my garbled voice brings up.

One further step. The room is bedlam. Petulia is coming out

of her seat, which I suppose is better than coming in your seat, with a hungry expression on her face.

Miss Didne-Dowel's eyes are open wider than dinner plates, and I can see straight down to her tonsils.

'But you're a biology teacher,' I say. 'You must have seen something like this before.'

'Yeah. The Post Office Tower,' shouts Petulia.

'No. Never in the flesh,' cries Anthea, falling to the floor in a dead faint, her sensible skirt riding up round her sensible thighs, revealing a neat line in very sensible pale pink satin bloomers, elasticated at the knees.

It is the last step that is my undoing, not that there's much left to undo. I stub my toe on the edge of the platform, and perform a graceful swan-dive forwards, rather like a certain nameless footballer entering the opponents' penalty area. But, that footballer doesn't have the sort of landing I have.

Right smack bang wallop on top of the prostrate Miss Didne-Dowel. I suppose I am lucky to get a soft landing, considering the state of Edgar. Looking back on it, I reckon that I can understand why Marilyn Thrustinne, attracted by the noise, should come into the lecture-room at exactly that moment, and might if you have that sort of mind, jump to entirely the wrong conclusion.

But I still don't see why she has to empty a fire-bucket of icy water all over me and then lay me out colder than a cod's Khyber with the blackboard duster.

'And we must be grateful that Anthea is an old friend and has agreed not to press charges on the understanding that we pay for her to stay for a month at a very expensive sanatorium. But, Mister May ... really. I'm sure you have a reasonable explanation.'

'Yes.'

'Well?'

'I think that what happened shows the danger of someone letting their work get on top of them!'

CHAPTER SEVEN

I have had more embarrassing moments. The trouble is that I can't actually think of any.

Although there is the time that I'm in the back row of the Beacon Cinema, Great Barr, with a local lovely named Judy Moody. Eventually married a short-sighted tree surgeon, who couldn't see the wood for the trees.

I can't remember what the film is, but it must have been a long time ago. Yul Brynner and Telly Savalas are both in it, and they've both got hair!

I've finished my choc-ice and I'm casually wiping my hands clean on her petticoat wondering if I'm going to get a slice of fish and finger pie. The way things are going, I really fancy my chances.

Moody Judy Moody suddenly takes the ice-lolly from her mouth with a noise like a blocked sink getting clear.

' 'Ere. Just what do you think you're up to, Jonny May?'

I'm doing a bit better than actually getting up to it. I'm more like inside the door.

'Nothing, love,' I hiss passionately. 'Just trying to get into your pants.'

I believe in the straightforward approach.

'Oh,' she says, moodily. 'If that's all, then save yourself the trouble. I got a spare pair in my handbag you can put on.'

It may be my natural modesty, but I'm still surprised to find that I'm not out of a job. Although, as usual, Jonny has done his little (!) best. I mean, I cured the first two patients. And what happened with the girls' biology class was hardly my fault. Perhaps, 'hardly' isn't the correct word to use in the circumstances.

But that evening, I am still sitting across the dining-table from Miss Thrustinne, and she is still speaking to me. Choice gems of conversation and friendliness like 'Pass the salt!' and 'Pass the pepper.'

I wish her the condiments of the seasoning.

Supper isn't my sort of meal. I reckon Marilyn must have hired a vegetarian cook. But I would be the first to admit that this supper has the true touch of gold.

Eighteen carrots!

First thing next morning I go for a walk round the neighbourhood, stopping off in a local park. Soon after I leave the clinic I have that funny feeling that (not *that* feeling, missus!) I'm being followed.

But I don't have any outstanding matters, unless you count Edgar. So it's not a creditor. And there surely can't be any paternity orders still following me around. Since it's not likely to be a fan of J. May after an autograph, then what can it be?

I twice stop and look in shop windows, trying to work out if anyone is really after me. All I see is a tallish lady in a long dark green coat with a hood. Sort of a Robin Hood.

When I get in the park I sit down on a bench and watch the squirrels tucking away their nuts. If you had to tuck your nuts in your mouth and climb up a tree you'd probably look as miserable as they do.

'Hello.'

By Brough and Andrews! A talking squirrel. Then I see that it is the lady in green who has joined me on the bench. Makes me feel like a magistrate, but where would I find one at that time in the morning?

'Hello.'

'Lovely day.'

'Lovely day.'

'Quite warm.'

'Yes. Quite warm.'

'But cooler than yesterday.'

'And maybe cooler than tomorrow.'

'Yes.'

The squirrels have all gone. They're probably as bored with that sort of time-wasting conversation as I am. I risk a sideways glance and see that the lady is quite pretty. Doesn't look the sort who might be on the game. Not the sort of game I mean.

'I've seen you before.'

By Shirl, Lock and Homes! Can it be another paternity order? Nowadays they always send them by post. Like my uncles give you postal orders for Christmas.

It can't be that. Nine months interest on a small deposit! Then what can it be? Perhaps the best thing to do is to ask her outright.

'You probably wonder why I've come up to you like this. Don't you?'

Now's my chance.

'No. Not at all. I often have pretty ladies coming up to me like this.'

'It's just that I'm sure I've seen you coming out of that big house in XXXXXXXX Street.'

Of course it's not called XXXXXXXX Street! Only I'm under a vow of secrecy about where it is and what goes on there.

'Possibly.'

'And I wondered if it was true about what goes on in there. It being a sort of special hospital for people with . . . personal things wrong with them.'

'My hips are healed. I mean my lips are sealed.'

There is nothing on this earth that would make Jonny break his word.

The mysterious lady offers me a five pound note.

'Well . . . No, I'm sorry, but I'm not open to being bribed.'

Not for a rotten fiver, anyway.

'I'm sorry, too. It's silly of me to offer you money. I'm sure that someone like you with medical training wouldn't be interested in money. Not on what they must pay you in that clinic.'

I should be so lucky!

She shuffles up the seat, nearer to me, glancing round towards some trees over on the right. Almost as though she's waiting for some kind of signal. As she moves I notice that she is wearing an odd flower pendant. It has a wire running from it down between her cleavage.

'I've spotted what that is,' I say, touching the thing. The flower, not the cleavage.

Her face goes whiter than my old man when his benefit is a day late. 'What do you . . .?'

'Joke. If I say I like it, and touch it, then I get a shock.'

'*You* get a shock! Oh, that's right. Ha, ha, ha.' Her laughter is not convincing. Perhaps she's annoyed that I spotted her little trick.

'Anyway, I can't tell you anything about the clinic.'

'So it is a clinic! Tell me more Mister . . .?'

'I'm May.'

'Then do.'

No comment.

'I'm Jonathan May, and I'm not telling you anything about what I do.'

She comes even closer and her hand drops casually to my knee. She wears a very nice perfume and I feel my senses tottering.

'You see, I have that sort of personal problem, that I talked about. When I meet a handsome man like you, I'd just do anything at all. Anything. And I need help.'

Jonny is ready and willing to help her. To help her do anything for me. But there is something about her that is not quite right. She seems uncomfortable, shuffling around, and looking over my shoulder.

'I'm sorry, Miss . . .?'

'Ra . . . Poone. Penelope Poone. I'm desperate. If you knew of somewhere round here that I could go to for help with my sort of problem, you would tell me, wouldn't you? Even if it was all a bit secret and hush-hush.'

Her hand has left my knee and is heading north in the general direction of Edgar. But I am a man of iron.

'Please.'

I have become a man of rust. Miss Poone has found my soft spot and is rapidly converting it to a hard spot. Then, across the other side of the park, I see Miss Thrustinne. I have promised her that I won't speak to strangers, and I worry for my job.

I leap upright, scattering fingers off Edgar like dandruff off a pole-vaulter's shoulders. Miss Poone looks shocked and also jumps up.

'What's up?'

Edgar was but he isn't any longer. In fact, he is actually a lot shorter.

'Touch of the old . . . shrapnel . . . can't help you, I'm afraid. Always someone there. Like to help but . . .'

I tearfully tear myself away from her, casting nervous glances at Marilyn who is happily watching the ducks. Happily for me.

'Mister May! I'll be here again, and I'll get in touch. I think we can help each other a lot. Mister Maaaaayyyyyy!'

I had been wondering what steps to take, and then I decide. Very long ones. Safely away from Miss Poone. I look back from a distance, and realise that I have probably got away from a loonie. Miss Poone is standing there by the bench, and she seems to be talking to herself. Actually, she seems to be talking into that joke pendant. Despite a slight yearning on Edgar's part, I am relieved to be clear.

When I get back to the clinic later that morning, I decide not to tell Marilyn about the brief encounter. As I go in through the gates past the lady Conan, I am sure that I spot Miss Poone sitting in a van on the corner of the road. I wave to her, but she ducks down. Perhaps I am mistaken.

Anybody can make mistakes. Now take Uncle Mick.

Please.

One day he spends his lunch time drinking his favourite

meal and takes a bit too much ballast on board, despite frequent visits out back at the 'Jolly Fisher' to pump ship. With some men drink goes straight to their heads. With others it goes to their legs. With Uncle Mick it goes somewhere else.

It increases his naughty thoughts, but reduces his ability to perform naughty actions. He lurches off in the general direction of the nearest passion-palace, which happens to be next door to a corn-merchant. A chiropodist.

In his well-Brahmsed state, Uncle Nick enters the wrong establishment, and collapses in a cubicle. He is just about sober enough to remember that he has to take off his clothes in a knocking-shop, then he falls asleep on the bed.

In comes a chiropodist's nurse, ready to cut his nails and trim his corns. Sees naked Uncle Nick flaked out on the bed.

'Oh.'

Up wakes Uncle Nick, wiping his eyes that look like a couple of sand-blasted boiled eggs.

'Oh,' repeats the nurse. 'I didn't . . . I mean . . . I expected to see a foot.'

Uncle Nick grins at her with all the charm of a broken urinal. 'Never mind, duckie. What's a few inches between friends?'

Lunch is not the friendliest meal around. Miss Thrustinne hardly talks at all to me, and I wonder if she might have seen me talking to the pretty Miss Poone. But I reckon it's probably just a hangover from the last three days. As far as I can see the first two days weren't too bad from the clinic's point of view, but what happened to me yesterday could have happened to any of you.

Any of you ladies, that is.

I read the paper while I masticate. Stops you going deaf. While I masticate my food. The meat is of a toughness approaching my mum's Sunday roast. With most families the Sunday roast often makes meals for two or three days. With mum it makes a useful doorstep for months.

Interesting article in the news today about how in these days of liberated ladies they are going to give hurricanes men's names instead of girls'. I suppose they're hoping that they'll peter out round the Virgin Islands!

Halfway through the steamed pud – Marilyn is like most ladies in that she obviously loves a chunk of chocolate dick – rather than the spotted kind, she puts down her spoon and stares at me.

'I do not see what a person like Elizabeth James sees in someone like you, Jonny. You're not unattractive. You seem to be not totally lacking in intelligence.'

Simper, simper, I go.

'Yet you behave like a half-witted Brummie tit who has to use both hands to find his own bottom and isn't capable of directing pee into a bucket.'

Unsimper!

'Flattery will get you everywhere with me,' I come back valiantly. And with some success as Miss Thrustinne actually grins at me.

'My God, Jonny! I feel like that dreadful man on television. You are awful, but I still somehow like you.'

'What's next? How about a great big fat juicy nympho who can't get enough of it?'

She closes her eyes like she's suddenly developed a nasty pain in the head. Or even in the neck. I suppose that it isn't the most tactful thing to say, but you know me. The moment I open my mouth I put my foot in it.

'I do have a new patient booked in for this afternoon, but I don't think that I'm going to entrust her to you. It's a case of great sensitivity.'

'That's for me.'

'You!' Her voice goes up several decibels. And I don't mean mean saying "decimals" with a bad cold.

'Jonny May, you have all the great sensitivity of a Military Policeman gobbing on an expensive Persian carpet.'

What a turn of phrase the lady has!

'Seriously though, what's wrong with this patient? I don't want to cure her by accident.'

Marilyn laughs, 'Jonny, I give up.' Promises, promises. 'I am grateful to you for those first two, and even though you're costing me a bomb.'

'Well?'

'Please remember what I've said to you about not talking to *anyone* outside about what goes on in here.'

I nod my head, keeping my fingers well crossed behind my back. I'm sure that the lovely Miss Poone doesn't count like that. She's just another disturbed lady who needs the magic touch of yours very truly. The trouble is that Marilyn is always around, otherwise I could get Miss Poone past the guard on the gate and slip her into the seductions suite in the basement for a touch of the meat injections.

'You will be dealing with someone of the blood royal, so discretion is even more important than usual.'

Royal! Someone of the blood royal!! My mind races over all the pissibolities. Possibilities. I have to admit that I start at the top and begin to work downwards. I mean, it can't be ... Her! ... Can it?

What about ... her? ... Perhaps all the riding around on horses has ... that would be something to put in my diary. Today I and Princess ...

'Sorry to interrupt your daydreams, Jonny, but the lady concerned is not from England.'

'Oh.'

I never really thought it could be either Her or her. Nice to ponder, though. Even the best of ponders end.

'She is the Princess Mora Lovinmi.'

'Where does she come from?'

'It's better we don't discuss that. Let's just say that the Princess is from a certain small country in the Middle East. And leave it at that.'

A real live Princess! The last time that I had the pleasure

with such a personage was in the fairy grotto at Stoppers of Knightsbridge. That encounter is there for all to read in 'Confessions Of A Shop Assistant.'

'What's her royal highness's problem? Worried in case the palace eunuchs suddenly start having themselves a ball? Or is the mink lining peeling off her toilet paper holder? It's all go for these rich folk.'

'Jonny, your Labour sympathy is showing again. Get the chip off your shoulder.'

'Why, is it leaving a greasy stain?'

'I simply cannot waste my time on your simple-minded attempts at humour. The Princess is to marry one of the richest men east of Basingstoke, and it is important that she should be fully experienced in matters of sexual fulfilment. And that is where you come in.'

I couldn't have put it better myself.

'I'm to teach her how to thingie?'

'Yes.'

'How long? And to stop you dragging out that freezing cold ruler, I mean how long do I have to teach her the many and varied arts of love?'

'One hour and forty-five minutes. If you need longer, then she can come back tomorrow for twenty minutes.'

'By the Inn and Out! All I can do in that time is tell her where it goes.'

'She is on an extremely tight schedule.'

'If it's as tight as that, I'm not sure I'll even get round to opening her ledger and making an entry.'

'That, Jonathan, is your problem. If you can tackle the Princess with the speed and success that you have shown in the last three days, then it will go some way towards restoring you in my eyes.' She glances at her watch. 'You will be in the basement in precisely twenty-three minutes, ready to go. You *will* be ready to go?'

'I'm always ready to go, Marilyn.'

'Just don't go too far.'

Reminds me of the time that I am with a young lady in her bedroom. Her mother is out at work and we have a few precious hours together; but I am not sure what kind of girl she is. Does she go? That's the question.

My fingers are carrying out some feel research, and there is no protest. So I decide to get it all out in the open (!) and ask her.

'If I do it all the way with you, will you go and tell your mum?'

'Why?' she replies. 'Do you want to do it all the way with her?'

I arrive in the basement room to find the canned music is still dribbling away from Antonio Manana and his Bounds Green Bambinoes. And the Princess is also there, sitting demurely on the edge of the bed, waiting for me.

But there is something that the wicked Miss Thrustinne hasn't told me. The Princess is not alone.

Mora Lovinmi is a lovely piece of exotic packaging. Standing not more than about five feet tall, wearing one of those veil things across her mouth. A yaksbash, or whatever they call them. A wispy piece of chiffon that looks as though it's a couple of pairs of knickers glued together. Pale pink. A small ruby stuck through the side of her nose. This is not a fashion that I like. Makes birds look like they're best of breed at Smithfield Show.

Although the weather's quite warm, the Princess is well wrapped in a long dark cloak, like a Dracula cast-off. And I would cast off Dracula as soon as look at him. Curly-toed sandals peep from under the hem of the cloak.

She is altogether a well-prepared dish, and I fancy getting my knife and fork stuck into her. This job isn't really work at all. This one will be as easy as falling off a log. And talking of logs, the other person in the room looks as though he – or it could be a she – is hewn from a log of wood.

Since there is lipstick round the lips I guess it might be

a bint, though you can never tell nowadays. She is built like Harvey Smith only not so slim. She is dressed in a somewhat similar fashion to the Princess, only more so. And without a jewel through her hooter. Probably couldn't find one big enough.

'Infidel dog!'

I look round for a woof-woof, but can see nothing. It is the big lady who speaks. It's easy to tell by the way her veil puffs out with the words.

'Prostrate yourself!'

Not on your Nelly! I'll put up with a lot to keep a job like this, but not the unkindest cut of all. I need my lustlance too much.

I suddenly notice that Gargantua has got a rather nasty-looking chopper in her hand. And I do mean 'her' hand.

Her chopper is about a foot long, which makes it about average as choppers go. But it has a gleaming polish to it and it ends in a very nasty point.

'Abase yourself before the daughter of the most high, before I remove your unworthy head from your unbeliever's shoulders with this scimitar.'

Well, if she puts it like that, I'm not going to argue with her. I am down on my hands and knees faster than a bending bishop. The Princess extends one foot from under her cloak, and I guess that I am expected to kiss it. Toes are not really my scene, and anyway I'm English. I shall not kiss the foot of some jumped up little tart from halfway round the . . .

I feel a nasty prick at the back of my neck. This doesn't mean I am the victim of some sinister skin-graft or organ transplant. It merely means that the big lady is resting the sharp end of her chopper on me. What a convincing argument that is!

I press my lips to the dainty little sandal with all the fervour of a true coward.

'You may rise and address the serene majesty of all of Asia. Patroness of all arts. Worshipper at the shrines of six continents. Bestower of all wisdom. Sister of the sun, moon and stars . . .'

'That will do, Fatima,' interrupts the Princess from behind her veil. She turns her hazel eyes on me as I clamber to my feet. 'Mister May, I believe?'

Who does she expect? Doctor Livingstone, perhaps? But one doesn't make that sort of joke to a Princess, specially not when her bodyguard is standing three inches from your back with the biggest weapon since . . . I can't honestly say I've ever really seen anyone with a bigger weapon than this one.

'At your service.'

'You will not speak to the serene majesty of all of Asia. Patroness of all . . .'

'Shut up, Fattie!'

'As your Highness wishes. Your words are my commands. To hear is to obey. Whatever . . .'

The Princess simply looks at her with those lovely eyes and the lady-in-waiting shuts up. Ignoring her, Mora Lovinmi smiles at me.

'You are to instruct us in the arts of love. Is that not so?'

I like the way that these royals use the royal 'we'. When they go to the royal 'loo'.

'Not exactly both of you.'

'I asked that we should be taught what is needful for a bride to know.'

'Yes. You, but not her.'

So confusing the English language for foreigners. The way she uses 'us' might make anyone less clever than me think I have to teach them both.

'You are to teach us both.'

'Both?'

'To be more precise, and I was taught during my time at Saint Hilda's College in your University of Oxford, that one should always be precise, you will teach Fatima and I will watch.'

I suppose I should have guessed. I've seen enough films set in these Arab sheikdoms to know that all these big nobs out there have loads of servants. And some of them test the food before the sheik eats. Some test wines before the sheik drinks. And some go before the sheik in case there's an ambush.

So, I guess it's reasonable that this Princess should have a servant to test out thingie before she tries it out for herself.

I have a touch of the shakes at the thought of all these sheiks. If only there was some way out of this one. I could wriggle out if I was the snake of Araby. Or if I could sheik a leg. Or even if I was able to twist and sheik.

But Fatima! Words fail me when I try to describe her. A cross between Norman Hunter and Mrs. Mills, but without any of the muscles of the one or the charm of the other. And I'm not saying which is which.

She has everything that a man could desire. Including broad shoulders and a fine moustache. It's no good, but Miss Thrustinne must find another sucker. And I do spell that word with an 's'.

'Why are you delaying, Mister May? There is very little time for the lesson, and I am paying a very great deal of money.'

The thought of what I've already cost the innocent Marilyn is nearly enough to make me change my mind. The cold edge of the scimitar across the back of my neck makes up the nearly part of the enough.

'I . . . I . . . suppose I'm ready. Perhaps Fatima would like to take off her clothes?'

Without that cloak I shudder to imagine what she can be like. Moby Dick in drag is the nearest my imagination can come to it. I reluctantly begin to take off my shirt.

There is a violent spluttering of what I guess is Arabic from Fatima, and the blade of her chopper whistles dangerously close to my left ear. And it is not whistling 'The Gypsy Rover' either.

The Princess barks an order at her and Fatima slowly lowers

her weapon. My weapon is about as low as it can get without actually going underground.

The guard of what looks from what I can see to be a nice body, promptly puts down her sword and climbs up on the vast bed, giving me what I can only imagine to be a wink from behind that veil. But she is still wrapped in the cloak.

'I can't do anything really unless she takes off her clothes.'

The Princess giggles. 'Mister May. The idea of Fatima taking off her clothes for you to demonstrate the skills of love-making would be funny if it was not so silly. She would tear any man apart who attempted to strip her. She is very old-fashioned and very stupid.'

I look across at Fatima who is now lying quite still on the bed. But she doesn't respond at all to the Princess's insults. Her royal highness follows both my glance and my thoughts. 'Don't concern yourself, Mister May,' she says with a dismissive wave of the hand. 'She is also quite incapable of understanding a word of English. Please go ahead with your lesson.'

'It'll be like playing the piano blindfold and with gloves on,' I say, wondering if I'm dreaming or not.

'Do it or I will have you fired. I may also have you blinded and set by the gate to beg as a lesson for others who defy me,' she says without a flicker of expression on her pretty little face.

'I'm not sure that our beloved Prime Minister would allow that,' I say.

'For our oil, your Prime Minister would do what we told him to.'

In two sheiks of a gnat's tail, I am off.

Since the Princess doesn't want her servant to strip, then I guess it might be bad form for me to peel, so I stay in my shirt and strides.

Fatima lies there as stiff as an iced banana while I stand by the bed pointing out what seem to be the main points of thingie. My hand once accidentally brushes one of the large lady's twin assets and her fingers twitch on the hilt of the sword.

The Princess is following my talk closely, and asks several questions.

'After you have touched *that*, then it is for me to respond by holding *this* and rubbing it up and down, thus?'

I don't need to tell you what 'this' is, do I? Nor do I have to tell you that the Princess is so keen a student of the art and science that she wishes to have everything demonstrated to her. Including Edgar. Who nearly bursts with pride at receiving the royal stamp of approval. I wonder whether I can have the royal coat of arms tattooed above him. 'By appointment to . . .'

'And after you have been squeezing these . . . can you also use your mouth upon them?'

'Yes. Yes you can.'

'Then you think things are ready for you to take that and put it in there?'

My face is gradually taking on the colour of a traffic light on 'stop'. This is not the sort of conversation that I can cope with.

'Yes. More or less.'

Her fingers again touch lightly on the subject so dear to my heart, and the response is immediate.

'But that is so very big.' Her eyes flash, and she looks very angry. Fatima senses the change in her mistress's voice and sits up on the bed grabbing at her chopper.

Just so long as she doesn't try and grab at mine.

'What's the matter?'

'You are trying to take me for a fool, Mister May, and I shall make you very sorry.'

'But I don't think you're half the fool you look, and even if you were, you still wouldn't act like the fool you are.'

Both of us stand there trying to work out what I've said. In the end neither of us can, so we ignore it and press on.

'It is obviously impossible for any woman to take in there what you have barely concealed in *there*.'

'Ouch!' On the last 'There' her serenity had poked me very hard in the front office with a lengthy fingernail, with the usual disastrous effect on poor old Edgar. I've never known anyone whose life is so full of ups and downs.

'Aha!' She laughs triumphantly. 'It is all a dreadful capitalist trick. It teaches me to kick against the pricks of you western tools.'

I back away in case she decides to actually start kicking against ... against anything.

'I don't know what you mean.'

'Yes. You wear an inflatable device beneath those decadent blue jeans. To make me seem a fool on my marital night. And you try to double the effect by a pack of damnable lies about how it is supposed to enter me there.'

As she spits out the last word, she pulls open the cloak, and I see that her underclothes are three-sue. See-through! No wonder she wears that cloak. Even in an English summer – that's when the snow melts as soon as it hits the ground – she would still be somewhat underclad.

'I promise you that it's no trick. It's not inflatable, and it does fit in ... in ... well, fits in.'

'Pfaugh! It is a foolish lie. I shall leave now and see that Miss Thrustinne and then my ambassador. It will be your fault when your country is oil-less within the month.'

'Tell you what.'

She pauses at the door, Fatima making a threatening gesture with her sword. 'What is it?'

'I'll prove it. You send out Queen Kong and I'll prove to you it's not a trick, and it does fit.'

'Impossible.'

They live very sheltered lives these Eastern ladies, don't they?

'Try me. If I fail, then you can do everything you said.'

Her eyes narrow. 'Very well, Mister May. Fatima will wait beyond the door and will come when I call. And it's not only your oil that risks being cut off.'

Talking of oil reminds me, in passing, of the Texas oil millionaire who goes in the dentist one day and says: 'Start drilling. I feel lucky!'

The door closes behind Fatima, and the potted music changes to 'Sheik, Rattle and Roll'.

'Now, Mister May. You have just five minutes to prove you are not trying to fool me and my wonderful and proud country.'

'It's Jonny. And I don't usually need that long.'

My strides hit the carpet with a resounding silence, and my shirt tails after it.

'How long, then?'

Those of you who know and love Jonny, will realise that there is only one answer to that. And I give it to her on a plate.

'Oooh!'

I help her off with her cloak and dagger, laying them both on the end of the bed. The Princess is fascinated by the . . . by the sight of Edgar beginning to take his usual healthy interest in her affairs. I can't understand the fastenings of her clothes, but she proves more than willing to help me out.

'But I still do not believe that it is possible for you to . . . Oh! Jonny! Oh, Jonny. How can you . . .'

The last word is muffled by a cunning application of my lips to hers. After a little hesitation, she responds. Does what comes naturally. She has a fine figure does this little Arab mare. I have never nibbled among such regal pastures before. Actually, they taste much the same as any other bird's boobs.

'And I have to do *this* to you?'

She's remembered her lesson well. She falters once, but I remind her that the answer is on the very tip of her tongue. The Princess is an ideal pupil and takes it all in.

And what more could a fellow ask for?

The royal rumpoe responds to some peasants revolting and trying to shove their way into hallowed grounds. Without even a 'Hello'. The main entrance is totally unguarded, and there is no attempt made to stop my ram from battering. Indeed, the Princess gives Edgar a big hand. Really, it's two little hands, but it all adds up to more or less the same thingie.

Although I worry a bit about Fatima creeping up behind me and letting me have it right in the tradesman's exit, I still manage to get my balls rolling in all directions.

Of course, you do know why snakes don't have balls, don't you?

Well, have you ever seen any snakes dancing?

It's a shame that things have to come to an end as fast as they do, but the Princess has a very tight schedule. She also has a very tight . . . wait for it . . . hand on her servants. Fatima doesn't come until the Princess calls her.

Oddly enough, the Princess doesn't call out until she comes. So I suppose there must be a moral there somewhere. If we had more than an hour in the afternoon, we could really get things together. Considering it is the first time for her, I wouldn't mind trying a thousand and one Arabian nights.

We manage to fit it in three times before the time is up. By then I am down, but I think she is pleased with the way I have held my end up for my country. And if not for my Queen, then for their Princess.

There is a crackling on the speakers and I recognise the voice of Miss Thrustinne. Sounding like the Chancellor of the Blankchequer when he finds his civil servants have mislaid five thousand million pounds from the Budget. Still, just add it on the bill for Concorde and nobody'll notice.

'I'm sorry to intrude, your royal highness, but your servant is concerned that she had heard nothing from without.'

She'd have heard plenty if she'd been within.

The Princess giggles and kisses me. On the mouth. Then solemnly shakes hands with Edgar. 'As we say in my country, Mister May. Well done thou good and faithful servant. Perhaps we might bestow on you the order of the Green Bison.'

'Perhaps the Pink Panther might be better.' And I also give her a farewell kiss. But not on the mouth. Not now we've been introduced.

'Thank you for coming, Jonny May.'

'Thank you for having me, your royal highness. It has been a pleasure, and I have never had a better pupil to teach the game of love. I envy your husband.'

'Jonathan. If you are ever in my country . . . I have a small palace in the hills. Nothing too grand. Four hundred eunuchs. I could steal away . . .'

I smile my thanks, but the thought of those glittering choppers puts me off it.

She dresses quickly, and I show her out, where Marilyn breathes an audible sigh of relief at the happy look on the face of the Princess. I give her a reassuring wink and walk back to my room, thinking I've saved England from another petrol price rise.

Arise, Sir Edgar!

Back in my room, I find that I've been singing: 'Oil be loving you.'

What a charming prince I might have made.

Before going down to eat, I see an odd thing through my window. There are some tall trees in the grounds, and I could swear that I see Miss Poone perched in one of them, staring at me through what look like a pair of binoculars. I blink, and when I look again, the mirage has gone.

Unless she is that keen on me, and so many ladies are, I am having delusions. I decide not to mention it to Miss Thrustinne, in case it upsets her.

But she is in a wonderful mood.

'Jonny. You've saved the day. The Princess left us more than enough to settle up all the debts and keep us in the black for weeks. Her only worry was in case any of this leaked out.'

'Don't worry,' I say, with a merry laugh. 'It's not like some contraceptives. If they split, then the maker's guarantee runs out.'

She actually laughs.

'Another patient tomorrow, Jonny. Right up your street, I should think.'

'What do you mean?'

'Wait till tomorrow. Are you tired out after this afternoon's efforts?'

'Not too bad. Why?'

She grins. The second bottle of wine has gone either to her head, or . . . 'Just thought you might come up to my room for a bit of extra homework.'

More of that later.

Like the sign says in the music shop: 'Gone out! Bach soon. Offenbach sooner.'

CHAPTER EIGHT

My condition the next morning reminds me of yet another hysterically funny story.

(Publisher's Note: Oh, where am I? Think I must have dropped off. Has he finished the story of that lady in the Chamber of Horrors? Jolly, jolly good. Must just close my eyes again and think about my next skiing holiday . . .)

There's this middle-aged spinster teacher. Not very pretty, and with something of a speech impediment. She is very keen on Norse mythology. All those lusty Vikings. One night she's reading alone in her little bed, immersed in the tales of these virile heroes.

Almost without noticing it, she finds herself praying to Odin. 'Pleathe thend me a thuperman!'

And since the Norse gods are kindly, this blond warrior appears in her room in a flash (!) of lightning, and they make mad passionate love all night.

As the dawn rises, the massively muscled hero prepares to leave her. 'Tell me your name,' she begs.

'I am Thor!' he thunders.

'Tho am I, but wathn't it marvellouth?'

No doubt you are all interested in knowing just what my boss is like between the sheets. After all, she is a very liberated lady. And after all she is tremendously well-informed in all matters of thingie. And after all she is a very attractive young woman, with everything in the right places and in the right amounts.

And after all she is . . . newted. Stoned. Potted. Sloshed. Three sheets under. Rather than under just one sheet. Pie-eyed. Brahmsed.

Drunk.

You may not know it, but booze has much the same effect on many ladies as it does on most men. It increases their desire but doesn't do a lot for performance.

Marilyn prances around the bedroom naked as a day-old chick, calling out that she's going to do me Salome's dance.

About the rest of her entertainment that evening, I think it's better if I just draw seven veils over it.

Sorry to disappoint you there. I'm sure that you are all gnawing at chair legs with frustration that you've missed out on a passage of naughtiness. Never mind, eh!

To cheer you up, here's a jest in time. You can read this while having your cold bath to cool off your passions. And it's not just your passion-fruits that get cold.

It seems that the Admiral's daughter – who is a shy and sheltered young maiden – falls hopelessly in love with a common sailor. Despite her father's concern and disapproval, and without even a 'Hello, sailor' they get married.

Three months later, the Admiral decides to heal the breach and invites his daughter round for a bite of supper. Although the subject is very embarrassing for him, he mentions it to her.

'Hrumph, m' dear. Your husband, being only a common sailor from the foc'sle, will ... probably ... only ... if you understand me ... be used to long periods without the company of a woman. Are you following me?'

'Closely, papa,' replies his daughter, puzzled.

'Well,' mumbles the old sea-dog (from Barking) his face assuming the bright hue of a port navigation light. 'They sometimes take their pleasure in ... sort of ... different way to others. So ... I wondered if you'd noticed anything like that going on?'

'Why no, papa. Everything is absolutely spiffing and marvellous.'

The Admiral goes redder than a Red Admiral and huffs off. Not to mention puffs off. His daughter, intrigued by her father's words, goes back home and asks her husband.

'Darling. Papa tells me that there is what you sailors call a "different way" of doing . . . thingie. Can we try it, do you think?'

Her husband shakes his head. 'Blurry 'ell! No. Why risk getting crowds of blurry kids?!'

It is at breakfast that Marilyn breaks the fast. I mean breaks the news of my next top-secret assignment. But first, the gargantuan lady guard comes pattering in with her size twelve wellies to report that she thinks someone's been trying to get into the grounds. And that she chased an intruder out over the back wall just after dawn.

'What was this person like?' asks Miss Thrustinne.

'A woman. Average height and build. Wearing a long green cloak.'

Over the other side of the table I am forcing down my fourth slice of soggy fried bread (like it should be) well loaded down with a couple of ladles of baked beans.

'A cloak?'

'Yes. Dark green. With a hood.'

A sort of Robin hood?

I cough out a mouthful of bread and beans, spraying the table-cloth, sending one bean skittering with unerring accuracy straight into Marilyn's coffee.

Beanz meanz mesz!

I get a funny look from Miss Thrustinne, but she is so used to my unusual eating habits that she ignores the outburst and carries on questioning the guard. Can it be Miss Poone? Must be. She must be so desperate, poor girl, to see me that she is taking all sorts of risks. I used to be crazy about liquorice when I'm at Saint Margarets Junior School, Great Barr, and I take all sorts of risks for it.

All sorts! Liquorice allsorts! Please yourself.

What do you think of the show so far?

(Publisher's Note: Rubbish!)

I am touched by Penelope Poone's desire to see me and

determine that I will help her. Marilyn has said something about going up west tomorrow. If I can get Miss Poone past the gate, then I will show her the ropes. And we can both get knotted.

'Have you seen anything funny around, Jonny?' asks Marilyn.

'Not since the last Morecambe and Wise Show. Unless you count that superb bit of comedy when that man tried to explain how they were building more Concordes because everyone they built lost more money and the only way to get that money back was to build more Concordes which would lose more money and then they'd have to build . . .'

'Thank you, Jonny. So you haven't seen anything at all suspicious?'

'Not since that man who said that the more Concordes they built the more money they'd lose and . . .'

'Shut up!'

'Sorry.' I get back to the more important business of seeing if I can break the British All-Comers' record for getting most baked beans on a single forkful of fried bread.

It is a little later that Marilyn finally tells me what my impossible mission will be for today.

'I hope you've recovered from yesterday with her royal highness,' she says bitchily.

'Yes. Getting to bed early last night for a good *sleep* helped.'

She has the grace to blush. The only person with more grace is that Prince of Monaco. First time I go there it's sunnier. But next time it's rainier!

'Well, today's patient will be exactly the sort of person you need.'

Not a real-life nymphomaniac?

'She is twenty-one. And her name is Edmonda Droppem.'

I once know a Brummie back home called Edmond. Typical sort of inhabitant of Birmingham. Goes to a drive-in movie. Doesn't like the film. So he slashes the seats!

'What's wrong with her?'

'Possible excess pituitary or hormonal inbalance, leading to hyperactivity of thyroid and concomitant over-indulgence in all forms of sexual activity, leading to neurosis state and feelings of anxiety and guilt.'

'Yeah?'

'Jonny, Miss Droppem is what is more commonly called a nymphomaniac.'

I overhear an interesting conversation in a pub the other day about a nymphomaniac wife. Couple of cheeries in their striped shirts and white collars. All carburettors and no regular fuel injection. One says to the other over their eighth whiskey of the evening: 'Bad news old boy.'

'What's that Rollo?'

'Your wife, old boy.'

'What about her, Rollo?'

'Think she's gone nympho.'

'Why?'

'Hear she's been going out with John.'

'That so?'

'Yes. Bloody woman's being unfaithful to *both* of us!'

I can hardly believe my luck. Every man claims that a friend of his knows a regular goer. Office bicycle. Can't get enough of it. Genuine nympho. But I've never met a man who's actually met a real nymphomaniac for himself.

Now, folks is the hour.

Marilyn gives me her usual briefing. After last night's shambles I'm not that interested in her briefs. Or lack of them.

Sounds like the cricket captain at school. All that about keeping a straight bat and playing yourself in. All I'm going to do is bowl a maiden over. And if she's a real live and kicking nympho, then I shall be surprised if there's much maiden left.

From all the old jokes about such ladies, I would have

thought that more practical advice would be to tie my ankles to the end of the bed.

'Edmonda Droppem?'

'Jonathan May?'

We shake hands. I smile pleasantly at the lady, keeping a weather eye open for any funny business. There is about as much funny business as in twenty-four hours of television comedy.

Miss Droppem is an easy on the eyeful. Average height, with longish blonde hair pulled back in two loose plaits. Deep green eyes like two warm limpid pools of . . . deep green water. Well, I'm not Poet Laureate, Sir John Betjeboots.

She has those sort of full red lips that makes one want to press hot passionate kisses on them. As one passes lower over the immaculate bodywork, I notice the beautiful twin headlights. Edmonda is wearing a thin blouse of some cottony material, and her headlights are trying to shine clean through the material.

Below the waist the lady wears a matching cotton skirt. What I'd like to believe are stockings, but the law of averages tells me are probably tights. Still, wouldn't mind topping her averages. With a taste of cream topping.

Good legs, without being actually world-beaters. As I'm very much a leg man, I'm a little disappointed.

'Do you approve of what you see?'

'Yes. Yes indeed. I'm sorry if I appear to be rude, but I've never met a . . .' Whoops! Nearly made a bloomer there. Tact, like Miss Thrustinne said.

'Met a what, Mister May?'

Must keep the subject off sex.

'Met such a lovely patient. Please tit down. Damn! I mean sit down. Sorry. Must think I'm a tit of . . . bit of a breast. Beast! Beast! Beauty and the beast. Must be losing my tits. Wits. Sorry. Everything's falling around me. Must pick up the tits. Bits! !'

This is awful. Once she gets the idea that I'm ravingly keen on thingie, then she'll probably start off and I'll be lucky to escape with my skin intact. Probably be down to my last threeskin.

'Terribly sorry, Miss Droppem. Lovely room this, isn't it?'

She nods, looking rather puzzled. 'Yes, Jonny? I can call you Jonny?'

'Course. Course you can. If the cap tits. Oh! If the cap *fits*!'

She is plucking at the buttons of her blouse and biting her lips. I have no experience of such ladies, but I am worried in case she begins one of her turns. And one good turn is bound to follow another.

'Tell me a little about yourself, Edmonda, then I can get closer to helping you.'

'Get closer?'

'No. I didn't mean that. Please stay that end of the sofa.'

'Can't we sit on the bed. I just *love* sitting on beds, don't you?'

'Cometimes. Sometimes! Yes. But tell me about your problem.'

'Jonny. It's like *this*!'

On the word 'this' she springs at me like a jet-propelled Shirley Bassey.

But I succeed in fooling her. I have sewn up the front of my trousers and her grabbing fingers meet solid resistance. I don't know about a stitch in time saving nine. But it certainly saves mine. Gently, I push her back on her side of the bed, using the opportunity to cop a feel of the headlights. Like the best of waiters, they are extremely well-tipped.

'No. Edmonda. I'm here to help you work out your problem.'

'Jonny. The best way of helping me with my problem is to **** me.'

The word spelled **** is not kiss. Nor is it pick or lick or suck. Though we are getting warmer. In fact, I'm getting positively hot under the collar.

'Just sit there quietly and try to describe to me what you feel when you're with a man.'

'All right. You tantalising devil! I just want every man I see to . . .'

'No! Please. I cannot bear to hear such words passing such pretty lips.'

'Do you really think they're pretty, Jonny?'

'Yes I do and . . . Get off! !'

'Sorry. Where was I?'

'Telling me how it felt.'

'Well. It's as though someone's sprinkled pepper right up my . . .'

'No! ! Edmonda! Please. I don't mean the actual physical parts. Though I'm obviously interested in your parts. I mean that . . .'

'Are you really, Jonny? Interested in all of my parts, I mean?'

'Yes. No. Possibly. But I have to keep stopping you in the knickers of time. Sorry. Go on.'

'You want to know what I feel, like in my mind?'

'In two words – pre cisely!'

'Right. It's funny. I don't actually enjoy the sex part. It's all over too fast. Like lighting the blue touch paper and then retiring immediately.'

Ah. Not to mention Ha. Have I stumbled on something? I check the bottoms of my shoes, but all is well. Must be the drains. No. Does this lady suffer from a complaint that I have read about in some of the non-dirty dirty magazines? What lots of blokes seem to have. Previous experience! That's not it. Pregnant strangulation? Hang on while I look it up in my little black book. And you Old Codgers can sod off, because I'm talking about a dictionary.

Premature ejaculation. That's it. Maybe Edmonda has this as well.

'Tell me more.'

'Well. I always hope that somehow it'll be better. It's so nearly marvellous. You know, like reading in a kid's book about that last one of the children of Hamelin who follow the Pied Piper. The one who's too slow. He glimpses this magic land within the mountain where all the others have gone, but it closes in his face, and he can't get in.'

'That's how you feel about thingie?'

'Yes. The door opens and I start to hear lovely music and it feels simply fantastic. Then they slam the bloody door on me.'

'And?'

'And I always hope that it'll be better next time, but I can't relax, and it never works properly.'

If she is a real live nympho, always grabbing at blokes, it doesn't take an Epstein to realise that most fellows are just going to want a quickie and away. So that must make it worse and so it goes on. What Edmonda needs, in the opinion of Doctor May, is a man who's going to take his time with her.

And where will she find such a man? I hear you all asking me.

He stands before her, is my reply.

'When I see a man I fancy, I want to tear off all his clothes, and then rip my blouse off, and throw off my skirt. Break the clasp on my bra and chuck it away. Pull down my tights, or get him to do it with his strong fingers, while he caresses me and kisses my breasts.'

Edgar is trying to go walkies, but finding the extra constriction of that cotton rather irritating. And so am I.

'Go on,' I say surprised at how hoarse my voice has become.

'I'm not boring you?' asks Miss Droppem, crossing her legs in a careless manner. I couldn't care less. He lied.

'Not at all. Go on.'

She goes on.

And on.

Next to doing it, I suss out that Edmonda also enjoys talking about it.

'After he's finished rubbing my breasts with his muscular fingers, he starts to lick me all over, running his tongue all warm and wet over my neck and body, slipping lower and lower while his hands excite me to an unbearable pitch of passion and excitement.'

It crosses my mind, while I cross my legs, that Miss Droppem might be reading too many books of the kind that would bring Mrs. W****house out in a hot sweat.

It's certainly bringing me out in a hot sweat and I am glad that I have the protection of a sure deodorant. I'd feel a right guard without it.

Note cunning plug slipped in there in hope of obtaining free samples.

'By now I'm ready for him to thrust his ...'

'Careful!'

'Into me. I rise and fall against him, and our hips grind together in a fusion of pleasure and pain. His white teeth nip at my pliant flesh, and I feel him impaling me to the soft mattress.'

This sounds to me like 'Virgin On The Ridiculous' by Christopher Hotpen.

'Then we mingle and merge in the supreme moment of sexual ecstacy, flowing and entwining together as we relax exhausted.'

There is a silence in the basement room, while I try to think of something to say to follow that.

I remember once that I enter a talent show at a holiday camp, and the bloke introducing me doesn't like me. So he gets up on the stage and says: 'Ladies and gentlemen. I have a very special announcement to make. In a few moments, on this very stage, you'll be able to meet Robert Redford and Paul Newman, with Raquel Welch.'

Of course, they all go spare at this, and there's about five minutes of cheering and stamping and whistling. The compère comes off the side of the stage and gives me a nasty wink, then goes straight back, holding up his hands for a bit of hush. He finally gets it.

'Ladies and gentlemen,' he shouts. 'I have bad news. I'm afraid that Robert Redford, Paul Newman and Raquel Welch have been unable to make it. But here's Jonathan May.'

Edmonda lies back, her face redder than a baked beetroot, her eyes not meeting mine.

'You must think I'm terrible, Jonny. To talk like that to you.'

'No. Edmonda, I really don't. But that's what you'd like thingie to be and it never is. So you keep going with every man you can to sort of hope that it'll all come true for you?'

This psychiatry is dead easy.

But after the talk comes the action.

'You may be right, Jonny. But what can you do to help me?'

Hands up those of you who think they can see what's coming. Not bad. The rest of you are just going to have to read on.

'That's right, Marilyn. I want you to send down two bottles of Southern Comfort. That's all I need. Then, with any luck, everything's going to be just fine.'

If I don't get a free case of Southern Comfort after this book, I'm going to give it up and start pushing Elderberry wine.

Actually, Southern Comfort is a marvellous drink. All warming and fruity.

Which brings me back again to Miss Edmonda Droppem and the basement of the clinic.

While I have been speaking to Miss Thrustinne on the intercom – which always sounds like a phone in your winter drawers – Edmonda has been simply sitting quietly on the bed, making an occasional half-hearted grab at the front of my trousers as I walk past.

The dumb waiter makes a lot of noise. As the two bottle of

Southern Comfort arrive, with two glasses. Now we've got the glasses, we can begin to make something of a spectacle of ourselves.

'What are we going to do, Jonny?' asks Edmonda as I pour out the first tumbler of the rich golden elixir.

'Drink this. That's good. Not too fast. After we've both had a nice slow couple of drinks, we shall begin what I hope will be a nice couple of slow . . . thingies.'

There's no thingie like a slow thingie, is what I always think.

Edmonda looks at me as though I've promised her the Crown Jewels, instead of the family jewels.

'I think I'll like that, Jonny.'

The thought of how much money I'm losing the clinic occurs to me. 'Edmonda? How much are you paying Miss Thrustinne for your treatment?'

'Let me see. Can I have another glass of the drink?'

'Sudden Bumthought? I mean Southern Comfort? here you are.'

'I'm paying fifty pounds per session. And Miss Thrustinne reckons that I'll need at least twenty sessions before you can help me properly.'

I begin to think that maybe Miss Thrustinne is a bit more concerned with the loot than her patients. That's a lot of bread for either talking about thingie or practising it. And I'm not seeing much of the money either.

It helps to ruminate into my glass of booze. And it doesn't bring hairs sprouting in the palms of your hand either

'Ready, Jonny?'

'Now, we're not going to rush it and . . . get your fingers off my shirt! It's going to be slow and gentle and . . . will you stop trying to get my trousers off! Thank you. That's what's at the root of your problem.'

She is so interested in my root that she is trying to nip it in the bud. And there is a nip in the hair. Not to mention a chink in the armpit.

'All right, Jonny. You're so masterful.'

It's my mastermind. And that reminds me of a joke on which I shall finish this chapter. But the time is not yet come. And, of course, neither have I.

It is time to cease drinking, before I start getting soft.

I shall now shuffle off my strides and begin the rescue operation. It is called 'Operation NAAFI'. Which stands for 'Nymphomaniacs Are Always Fairly Inhibited.'

But the damned cotton is in the way, and in the end I have to have a slash. Sometimes you do. I find that it helps if you have a good slash first. Don't you, folks?

At last the final thread parts and falls to the floor. Where I lose the thread, but as my jeans are now round my ankles I don't reckon it matters that much.

'Now, Jonny. Now!'

'There is a short tale – like a hamster's – that I want you to remember, Edmonda. There are two bulls in a field. One old and experienced and the other very young. In the field across the valley there are twenty pretty young heifers. The young bull paws the ground and says: "Let's charge over there and do a couple of those cows!" To which the older bull replies: "No. Let's *walk* across and do *all* of them." Understand?'

She nods.

I remember the words of her fantasy, and I do my best to live up to it, but at a more reasonable pace.

So away we go . . .

I allow Edmonda to rip off my clothes, having cunningly undone the buttons first. Edgar enjoys this and expands to fill the space available. Thus proving Jonny May's First Law of thingie that says that an Edgar will always seem to expand to fill whatever hole is available to him.

Although physical violence is not in my bag, I do what Miss Droppem wants, and pull off her blouse, tearing it across the front with a satisfying noise. The skirt goes the same way, and I kick it into the corner, using a technique I model on the way my old man used to drop-kick mum into the airing cupboard on a Friday night.

'Yes, Jonny. More.'

The bra is only a wisp of silk, and it parts under a good tug. She falls back on the huge bed, mouth slightly open, fingers hanging on Edgar tighter than Micky Droy to an advancing striker. I gently disengage him, and then take out my hatred on tights in general by tearing down hers, and shredding them into flakes. Makes a change from shredding wheat!

Miss Droppem is wearing a fairly ordinary pair of panties. Sorry to disappoint you lovers of exotic knickers, but not all birds wear them. And I'm not going to make anything up in these books. Edmonda's underwear is pale blue. Bikini pants, with little black spheres on them.

I decided to leave them on for just a little bit longer. Edgar decides that he isn't going to wait for very much longer, so I try and think about something amazingly boring like television chat-show comperes. It works, and I feel less hearty. Not to mention less Parkinson, and lot less Nimmo.

'Kiss my breasts,' mutters Edmonda.

Blast! I had forgotten she said that when she went through her fantasy. Still, I don't mind and tit my teeth ..., grit my teeth and we move on.

Next on the agenda of the meeting is the licking all over part. She has obviously bathed within the last two or three weeks so I don't mind that either. Edmonda keeps grabbing at my fingers, trying to draw them nearer to her passion-pad, panting like a steam engine. But I hold off actual contact, as part of my plan to keep things bubbling and simmering rather than coming straight to the boil and making a mess all over the top of the stove.

To keep her ticking over I make a few magic passes across the front of the knickers, which produces electrifying results. Like a hot-crotch bun.

The warm and wet tongue she wanted – I've done that. And I'm keeping my hands away for the present from the exciting her to an unbearable pitch of passion and excitement bit.

The most unbearable pitch I ever played on was in Red House Park, Great Barr. In the cricket season you had more sharply rising balls there than in six months at the Raymond Reviewbar .

'Now. Come on Jonny. I want to feel it right inside. Come on! Please! I can't wait for it to get any longer.'

There is some evidence of forcible entry, but with the approval of the householder. Having got Edgar all charged up, I don't think that Edmonda is going to hold it against me. But she might hold it against herself.

It is now that the cunning part of Jonny's operation gets going. Since Miss Droppem suffers from having too much too soon too often, I slow it down and don't let her have what she wants.

'Please!!'

But I press her to the bed – I'm one of the gentlemen of the Press – in a folding body-slam and keep up the three-finger exercises. It all turns out to be rather too much for the poor lady.

'Honest, officer. She just came off in my hand. Three times.'

Only when she's all limp and shuddering, rather like my old man after a night at 'The Flog and Nightgown', do I finally carry out the last part of her fantasy. The bit where she gets impaled and our hips grind and my white teeth nip at her pliant flesh and all that stuff.

At last we merge and mingle in all the sticky juices and fall on the bed exhausted. Just like she said. And it has actually worked.

'That's the first time that I've ever done it properly, Jonny. It was wonderful. Oh, it was so good. It was like I always hoped it would be. Ooooh. It was *so* good!'

She sounds like Lee Marvin in 'Cat Ballou' after he's just shot his brother.

Me, I've just shot my bolt.

But the horse is still in the stable. Eager for another ride as well. So we gallop towards the sunset, and hit the hay at about the same moment.

Afterwards, while we both sip at a couple of medicinal Southern Comforts, Edmonda rolls over and touches me very gently on the . . . near the . . . Edgar.

'That was fantastic, Jonny. You're the first bloke that ever really took any trouble over me. You're really marvellous. I can see why they got you to work here. I reckon you could cure any girl of anything.'

'You reckon you're cured?' I ask, my pleasure mixing with horror at the thought that this continued amazing success rate is going to be the ruin of Miss Thrustinne's clinic. Which also means the ruin of yours truly. I've only had this job for four days so far. Normally, as my many fans will know, I manage to last a bit longer.

The best part of a year at the exclusive store in Knightsbridge. Stoppers. And several months in most of my other jobs. So this could be a record.

It is fair to say that Miss Thrustinne is not pleased at the news, though she pretends to Edmonda that she's delighted to hear of my miracle cure. I am beginning to suspect that maybe the beautiful Miss Thrustinne is in this for more than just being nice. If she's in it for the money, then she is not going to be able to keep me working for her for much longer.

And she tells me so.

'I cannot afford another cock-up,' she says.

After all the exercise that Edgar had been having in the last three or four days, I don't think that money would make a lot of difference in the cock-up business.

'I am going up to London tomorrow, and I shan't be back until late. You can have the day off, as there are no more patients booked in yet. But you are not to leave the premises. Is that clear?'

'You have my premise. I mean promise.'

Her voice is colder than an Eskimo's big loo.

I get that old familiar feeling that my days are numbered.

And that the numbers don't run much higher than about seven. Still, not a bad little run for the money. That is, if I'd been paid at all.

'And keep your eyes peeled,' (what a revolting thought that is when you think about it) 'There may still be intruders around.'

Miss Poone. It will be interesting to wait and see what tomorrow brings. . . .

But before we toddle off to the land of Zzzzzz, here's that small joke about Masterminds I promised you a few pages back. Here's a bit of useless information first. On the way to Los Angeles, there is a road called 'Zzyxx Road.' Just thought you'd like to know.

Here's the joke.

There's this aeroplane flying across some mountains when its engines start to fail. Better than some British planes whose engines simply fail to start.

Captain comes over the intercom. 'Sorry passengers. I and my co-pilot have done all we can but I'm sorry to have to tell you this plane is doomed and will soon crash to earth from ten thousand feet. We are bailing out. The parachutes for passengers are in the luggage compartment. Good luck and claim your refunds from your travel agents on returning to London. Goodbye!'

They look out of the window, and see the parachutes of the crew drifting safely away.

They rush to the luggage hold and there are the chutes for them. But there is one big problem. There are five passengers and only four parachutes. Well, it's an off-season package tour. The plane's so old it's actually got an outside lavatory!

'I think that I should definitely have one of those parachutes, because I'm a bishop, and I am responsible for the guidance of all my flock,' says the first passenger.

The rest agree that's fair, and he grabs the pack and jumps.

Four passengers and three parachutes.

The four men are a doctor, a man on a hiking holiday, a writer and an unemployed labourer from Birmingham.

The doctor speaks next. 'Because of what I do, I think that I must have a parachute so that I can carry on saving life on earth below.'

The rest agree that he's given them a sound argument, and off he goes.

Three men and two parachutes.

The labourer clears his throat. 'I reckon I must go next. I'm representing my city in "Mastermind" as the greatest brain in Birmingham. That's so important that you must let me jump next.'

The other two nod their heads, and he grabs a pack and jumps through the hatch.

The writer looks at the hiker. 'Looks like one of us is in big trouble.'

Not really,' grins the hiker. 'The brain of Birmingham just jumped with my rucksack!'

CHAPTER NINE

I don't just want you to think that all Brummies are thick. A mate of my old man is working on a building site. When he trips over and falls down this great big, hundred foot deep hole.

Foreman hears the crash and comes running over. Looks down the hole and shouts out: 'Are you all right down there? Is anything broken?'

My old man's mate's voice floats up through the dust and darkness. 'No. Nothing's broken. There wasn't anything down here to break.'

I stay late in bed. It is well-known that Jonny is not an early riser. Anyone who wants to leap out of a warm bed just to catch a worm must be right round the twist.

I hear the front door slam shut, and watch from behind the curtains as Marilyn Thrustinne walks down the drive towards those heavy gates. I notice she too has a heavy gait, but that might be because I have borrowed her talcum powder to make Edgar a little lovelier every day.

Apart from the stormtrooperess on the front doors, this means that I more or less have the place to myself, And I can bring in Penelope Poone. Solve her problem, which sounds remarkably like Miss Droppem's and bring in a bit more money to make Marilyn love me more. And keep me on.

One minor problem.

Where do I find Miss Poone?

I have no address and no number. Perhaps if I go to the park where I first met her? I can sneak out the back way, over the fence, and get away.

But first things first.

Breakfast.

Damnation!

A note from the cook which says simply: 'Miss Thrustitte says you aren't to have nothing seeing as how you never get up out of bed in time for anything so you don't get nothing at all.'

Charming.

May her omelettes wither!

Freedom. It isn't at all hard (!) and I creep through the undergrowth and even some of the overgrowth, reaching the high wall without being spotted. Honestly. All this secrecy is absurd. Anyone would think that there were television crews lurking behind every wall, just waiting to sneak a story about a sex clinic.

I drop down in the road ready to make my way to the park and look for Miss Poone.

'Hello Jonny!'

I jump several feet in the air as the voice seems to come from right up my rear entry. I shoot round and there is Miss Poone, lurking behind the wall. I spot three or four men haring off down the road towards a parked van and I wonder for a moment who they can be. But it's obviously nothing to do with me, so I turn all my attention to the ravishing Miss Poone. Who has changed her green coat and hood for a dark red cloak and hood.

'Blimey! You gave me a turn!'

'I've been waiting in the hope that you might be able to give me a turn, Jonny, darling.'

How can I resist? There is a nagging doubt that this lovely lady can really have been waiting here at the most secluded part of the clinic's grounds for a couple of days just on the off chance that I might appear. But girls do things like that for me, so I remove the nagging doubt.

And I guess that the tripod thing those three men are carrying down the road is probably something to do with surveying.

Probably.

'Can we get inside there, Jonny?'

'Well. . . .'

'Please. We've been . . . I mean that I've been looking round the outside, but there's a real dragon on the front gates, and she says there are guard dogs inside and we . . . I don't want to have my knickers ripped off.'

'No?'

She rests her hand on my arm, and I get one of those electric flashes that make me into a jumping Jonny flash.

'I mean that I don't want to have my knickers ripped off by any of those dogs. But if anyone else came along with the right sort of offer. . . .'

She leaves her promise dangling longer than a Party political broadcast.

'There aren't any dogs. If you climb over the wall here, you can get through the woods to within a few yards of the house. My boss is out, so I can get you in.'

The broadest of smiles beams across Miss Poone's face, and she half-turns as though there is someone she wishes to share the good news. Or the black magic or the milk tray.

Although there is nobody in sight, except for a small plain van parked right down the end of the road, Miss Poone is so delighted that she gives an enormous thumbs-up sign to the morning air.

'Wonderful, Jonny. So we can all get in safely and no questions?'

'Hardly *all*, Penelope. Just you and me.'

'Of course. Look, Jonny, I have to make a quick telephone call. I . . . Errrr . . . have to ring up my mother and tell her I've got the knitting needles she wanted me to get for her. Won't be long. You hop over the wall, and I'll see you on the other side.'

Seems fair enough, so I begin to clamber up the surface of the brickwork. It sticks out in places so it's easy to get a good hold. I'm sure some of you ladies will know what I'm talking about!

I'm sitting on top of the wall . . . just rolling along, just singing . . . when Miss Poone returns. And hisses up at me like a snake in the grass. Which I am sure she isn't. I pride myself on being rather a good judge of character.

'Jonny?'

'What?'

'Another thing?'

'What other thing? What's wrong with the thing I've already got?'

'Nothing. But this room, we're going to . . . to do, you know what?'

'Yes. And I know how. What about it? Hurry up. This wall is cutting into my aspirations.'

'I suffer from a sort of claustrophobia. Has it got windows we can open?'

I think back to the basement. It's difficult to remember what the rest of the room is like, but I do recall there is a big bed there. Then I remember. Although it's a basement, there are huge double windows opening on to a sort of sunken courtyard at the back. Surrounded by a shrubbery of rubbery plants.

When I tell her this, you'd think that I've told her she's going to get a chance at 'Sale Of The Century'. Incidentally, as I write this, there are appalling rumours that this most wonderful programme might be ending. I cannot believe it. It's like being told that the sun isn't ever going to rise again. If these rumours prove true, then join me in writing to the T.V. people to get them to reverse their ridiculous decision. Don't forget.

Meanwhile; back at the sex clinic. . . .

I am over the garden wall, waiting for Miss Poone to finish calling her mum about the knitting needles. She has been so long that I am beginning to get the needle.

At last I hear her coming down the road. Well, some women do make a lot of noise when they're coming. It's those high-heeled boots they wear. There seem to be some others with her, as I'm sure that I can hear other feet and other voices. Just as I am about to clamber back up again for a butcher's, her leg appears on top of the wall.

By Brend an' Foster! This girl is athletic. She climbs up faster than I can climb down, and she is hardly breathing hard at all. Not a single pant. And I can see all as she is sitting on top of the wall. Even if I'd had a bunk-up I don't reckon I could have done it any better.

Since a bunk-up is what I hope for, I offer her my back to jump down on. I feel a bit of a heel.

Two heels actually. Right in the middle of my spine. I shall be marked for life. But she is down and we both make our way towards the clinic, creeping through the bushes like a couple of Cheyenne. I used to know a girl in Brum who wouldn't let anyone see, let alone touch. We called her 'Shy Anne', as well.

I manage to open the door a crack, and we slip through. Morgana the Mighty is still patrolling the front drive and we have the whole of the house to ourselves. Penelope waves me on ahead to show her the way. Later I shall show her as many ways as I can. The catch slips on the door behind me with a loud click. Funny that. I could have sworn that I locked it properly!

Just as I am about to go back and check, Miss Poone is right behind me. 'Now we're really alone,' she breathes in my ear, letting me feel her hot breaths. Yeth!

'Which way now?'

'Down here. Left, and then on down the stairs. It's the first door on the right.'

'Left. Down the stairs. First door on the right. Fine. Come on then.'

Although the house is empty of people, like all big places, there are still odd noises. And I can tell you that I speak from experience of lots of very big places. Penelope holds on my hand tightly as we creep along, gasping at the size and fitting of the Passion Suite.

'Jonny! I honestly never guessed that it would be as big as this.'

For a moment, I wonder if my flies have dropped out again, but it is only the room she means.

'Are those the french windows?'

'Yes. Big and heavy and still easy to open. Like most French widows!'

I pause for laughter. I have heard more laughter at a conference of grave-diggers. Penelope is concerned with struggling to get them open.

The windows!

'Can I give you a hand?' I asked, playing the part of the gentleman to perfection.

'As wide as you can, please.'

'There.'

She stands in the opening, peering out, looking round the courtyard, seeming happy with what she sees.

'Jonny? What's your role here?'

'My role?'

'Yes. How do you earn the bread?'

'Ah. A bread-roll! I'm sort of an assistant, helping out with ladies who have problems. Problems like you.'

'I don't have any. . . . Oh, yes. Of course. My problems. Yes.'

She seems to be more interested in chat than thingie, but I reckon that it is probably nerves. Miss Poone is not in very good shape. Well, her shape itself is fine. And very nicely distributed. But she is on the edge of some kind of nervous breakdown. And I don't have a breakdown wagon.

I slip out for a very quick session of elevating Edgar at the earthenware, and when I come back she is talking to herself. Or, rather she is talking to that funny pendant.

'Resting,' I think she is saying. And then she starts to count into it: 'One, two, three, four, resting.'

I cough, and she leaps round, looking pinker than I remember her.

'Oh Jonny. You've been quick.'

She says it in such an odd way that it gives me the hump. Carry on like that and I'm not going to hump her after all!

'Sorry, I'm sure. But I never was much of a Southend.'

'A Southend?'

'A long peer.'

I notice that she has switched on all the lights while I'm out of the room. Now Edgar and me prefer a bit of dimness, so I start to switch them all off, but Penelope stops me.

'Jonny. Do you mind if we have the lights left on? Only I can't do it at all if there's no lights.'

'I'm only going to turn some off. It's like a television studio in here.'

'I wouldn't know, Jonny. I mean I wouldn't know what a television studio looks like. Honestly, I don't know. Truly I don't.'

'All right, all right.'

I can't stand people who go on about the same thing. I remember that Uncle Angus used to keep going to the doctors, always complaining that he'd got wind. After the eighty-ninth visit the doctor presents him with a kite!

Still, if the patient wants bright lights, then she can have them. I turn up the volume of the wall to wall music, but that's wrong as well.

'No, Jonny. I'm sorry to make such a fuss, but everything's got to be right for me. And if there's a lot of noise it means that we . . . I can't do it properly. Could you turn it down a bit?'

'I turn it down a bit.

'A bit more, Jonny?'

I turn it off.

Any more of this and I shall be turning it in!

Penelope sees that I am getting choked off with things and comes over and gives me a hug, pulling my mouth to hers, and slipping the tongue into top gear. Edgar responds like a bull in a trouser shop.

'Can we get started?' she asks.

(Publisher's Note: I'd rather know when we're going to get finished.)

And I'd like to know when he's going to go and get knotted.

He should know how. He spends enough time chasing after boy scouts!

Although, as I'm getting near to my climax (!), I suppose this is as good a place as any to remind you about the joke competition. Send them in to me at Sphere Books, 30–32 Gray's Inn Road, London, WC1. To reach me before Easter, 1977, so get a move on. The winner will get a tenner, which by Easter, 1977, might be enough to buy you a bar of chocolate and a newspaper.

But all of you who send in jokes will have your names mentioned in the Dedications pages at the front of a later book. And don't forget the frillies, ladies.

One thing that I notice about Miss Poone is that she seems to have difficulty with her memory. At first she claims that she can't do it at all. But the first session settles that one for her.

So then she says that she remembers now. It isn't that she can't do it. It's that she wants to keep on and on and on and on.

Which is fine by me, and Edgar doesn't object. I know that he will not let me down and will manage to keep his end up. And he does. Keeps it right up for so long that I worry about his health. But Miss Poone rescues him and gives him the kiss of life, while I pay tender attention to other matters. Which also turn out to be tender as well.

Considering the brightness of the lights which makes it possible to see every hair on ... the back of my hand, it is not a bad bit of therapy. While we are tangling together I also find myself sharing Miss Poone's delusions. For instance, I think I hear an odd whirring noise. Perhaps Edgar needs a new battery is my first thought, but it can't be that as he is going well inside, outside and exide.

Then there is the sound of something falling out in the

courtyard. I start up, but Penelope is finishing down so I let it pass.

'Must be a pigeon dropping a message of love,' comments the lady when I draw her attention to it.

I have always thought that no pigeon yet hatched was big enough to drop solid steel messages of love, but that's by the by.

And there's the ear-rings. One of Miss Poone's fancies is that she strips off all the necessary parts, but keeps on her blouse. And all of her jewellery. The pendant, and a pair of rather large ear-rings, which seem to fit *into* her ears rather than hanging on the outside.

During the second, or it might be the third, thingie session, I am busy with my teeth, burrowing around her lobes, when I accidentally nip off one of her ear-rings. And it is at this point that I have a strange hallucination.

I seem to hear a tiny voice speaking to me from her ears. It says: 'Hurry up. She'll return soon.'

Return? But she's not going anywhere, except up and down rather fast.

Maybe it's an omen. There's no place for an omen. Like hearing that 'Turn again, Whittington. Thrice Lord Mayor shall you be.' Rather than admit that I'm going round the bend in a coach and four, I decide not to mention it. Apart from hastily putting back the ornament, Penelope doesn't say anything.

Just moans a little.

Talking about moaning, makes me remember the time that I'm in our local doctor's. Not the witch-doctor. He flew off in a mumbo-jumbo jet!

Our ordinary doctor. I'm sitting in the waiting-room, as I have been for the past three or four hours, when out comes a nun, crying her eyes into a big white handkerchief. I'm next in, as it happens guys and gals, and I ask the doc what's been happening.

'Just told that nun there that I thought she was pregnant.'

'Heavens to Murgatroyd! Is that true?'

Doctor laughs. 'No. But it cured her damned hiccoughs!'

Penelope is well cured of not being able to. I am up to my armpits with work at this clinic. What surprises me is that she seems to be able to both do it and talk about it at the same time. She is a mine of questions.

'Who owns the clinic? How many people? How much does she charge? What sort of staff? What sort of qualifications? How long have I been there? How often do I have to . . .? How much am I paid?'

It is fair to say that Miss Poone is a lot of talk and no knickers. Aforementioned panties hanging on the corner of a picture of a very fat lady on a very thin motor-bike.

Although I find it hard even to talk and chew gum at the same time, I do my best to satisfy her curiosity. But I don't like talking shop, and specially not curiosity shop.

It is only afterwards that I recall the warning of Miss Thrustinne about giving away secrets. I'm not exactly giving them away. I am charging her. Though I miss a couple of times. Anyway, there's nothing at all suspicious about Miss Poone. Is there?

What do you mean? Why should I have put clue and clue together and made four?

Sorry, but I don't know what you're on about. Penelope Poone, as far as I'm concerned, is as honest as any politician. I mean, it's not as though I'm getting fed up with the way Miss Thrustinne treats me and exploits the patients. Is it? Because, if that was so, then I suppose an evil-minded person might suspect that I know something sinister about Miss Poone, but am ignoring it just for my own ends.

Since none of my readers are evil-minded then I'm sure that none of you will think that. You'd probably rather go on thinking that Jonny's not all that bright.

Wouldn't you?

Rotten lot!!

Although it is rather odd when Penelope suddenly stops the horizontal exercise she's been doing so well, cocking an ear, which is better than earing a . . . Never mind.

All I hear is a bird cry.

Nothing unusual about that.

I often hear owls hooting at one o'clock on a lovely sunny afternoon. Without any more ado, and a lot of a'don't, we tear ourselves apart. Our parts are apart at last.

'Must go, Jonny. Thanks for a lovely time and I'm sure we'll meet again. You've been terribly helpful to me. You'll never know how helpful.'

A quick kiss on the cheek and there she is.

Gone.

I suppose she's got to go and get her mother some more knitting needles.

Three minutes later, Marilyn comes blazing in like an Icelandic gunboat and gives me a nasty blow right in my crispy cod balls.

Looking back on it, I suppose that if I'd wanted to keep Penelope's visit a secret, it would have been wiser to have removed that pair of panties hanging on the picture of the lady with the little chopper stuck between her legs.

And it seems that Miss Poone was spotted as she climbed back over the high wall by the delightful Gestapo lady as she patrolled the grounds. Which goes to make it grounds for separation.

Mine and the clinic.

After I recover from the blow to my assets, Miss Thrustinne calls me up to her pink-doored room. By now I really don't give a monkeys about things. I reckon when I start that this is going to be just the job for me. But I have already decided that getting no pay is a sore point. And what is more I am getting a sore point with no pay.

Marilyn has not forgotten that she did less than well in the bedding handicap. Her handicap proving too much for her. It isn't that I repelled her advances, because I encouraged them. It's more what happened to her advances. They turned into retreats. Her assault had no pepper to it, though I was keen as mustard.

Despite her figure, Miss Thrustinne really turns out to be a big flop.

I haven't forgotten it, and neither has she. Her first words lead to a shrinking feeling in the wallet.

'Jonny. After some thought, I have decided that I simply cannot afford to have a one-man disaster like you working for me. My sole reason for hiring you was that I needed a man who could handle the ladies. To my regret, and for reasons that I personally do not understand, you have been both too successful, and yet too much of a failure.'

It's that good old Bob Dylan feeling I was talking about earlier.

Marilyn, having given me the very bad news, goes on to give me some good news. It seems that Liz James has not hit it off with the Frog film-maker. Nor has she had it off with him. And she is coming back to England in a few days instead of staying in gay Paree for three months. So there will be somewhere to lay my head.

Among other things.

'So I don't really see why you shouldn't make like a fisherman and sling your hook right now.'

'That's not very friendly, Marilyn,' I say plaintively, though I'm neither very surprised nor very disappointed. I can read the writing on the wall. I should be able to, I wrote most of it myself.

'This clinic needs two things to make it go. One is lots of stupid women with imaginary complaints to cure which they are happy to pay me large sums of money. And the other thing is that I need complete secrecy for several weeks until I'm coming good.'

From my one night stand, and it was not a grandstand, I

doubt if Marilyn will ever be able to come good. Perhaps a few days in a good clinic . . .?

'You have blown the first, and I am inclined to think that you've been up to something behind my back.'

Well, I find it's a waste of time trying anything up her front.

'I will ask you again. Who was that woman I nearly caught with you this morning?'

'That was no woman.' I wait for a witticism to claw its way up out of my throat, but nothing happens at all and I stand there like a spare neurotic at a sex clinic wedding.

'Well?'

'Fine thanks.'

'That's cheap, Jonny. And I certainly didn't think that you were cheap.'

'The only things cheap round here are the baby chickens. Anyway, I must be cheap. Since you haven't paid me a penny yet.'

'A penny! What would you do with a penny?'

'Spend it. I'm bursting. So, if that's all . . .? I guess this means the bullet?'

'I'm afraid that I shall have to dispense with your services, if that's what you mean.'

That's what I mean, all right. No pay! Still, I've had a fair portion of free thingie. And some food. Even a laugh or two, and not many jobs offer all that. And Liz James on her way back from the land of the Awful Tower.

I decide to leave with a sting at her piece of tail, which should also hit her piece of mind.

'Marilyn?'

'What?'

'Ladies come here to you who have problems with a decent sex life?'

'Yes. Why?'

'Like it says in the Good Book. Physician, heal thyself first.'

With that crushing remark – remarkable how crushing she finds it – I exit smartly, closing that pink door behind me for good.

And head for Notting Hill once more.

Like I say. It's no big blow to lose a job. Not like losing a blow-job, after all. Nor is it a shock at all. Not like a shock that a mate of mine suffers.

He leaves for the office on time, like he does every morning, when he discovers he's forgotten something. His briefcase, packed with all those vital documents. Not to mention his crushed haddock and marmalade butties.

Lets himself in and walks upstairs. There, stark naked, is his wife in the bedroom, standing on the scales, with her rear elevation presented to him. He smacks her on the bottom and asks her: 'How much today?'

Without even looking round, she replies: 'Two pints of milk and a pint of double cream as usual.'

I spend three or four days catching up on movies that I've missed and lounging around Liz's flat waiting for her to return. She's due back Sunday, and on the Saturday I'm lying out with the cans on, soaking up Doctor Hook. Like 'Whispering' Bob says on 'Whistle Test', they're the group least likely to succeed with any girl's mother.

The telly is on and there's some sort of well-meaning and very boring programme on. The hostess is a new lady that I have read a lot about in the papers, but have never seen. Her name is Maudlina Moone. I can only just hear the telly through Doctor Hook, but it seems to be another of those tedious exposé programmes.

I half-watch with half an eye. Which makes for a quarter viewing. It seems to me that Miss Moone is vaguely familiar, then I see something that perks me up. And Edgar too. There is Miss Moone with nothing on at all, grappling with a naked young man on a vast bed. What a coincidence. There is a picture on the wall that is exactly like the one in the basement of the clinic. The fat lady with the.... Yes. That one.

Isn't that a coincidence?

It is so amazing that I actually turn down 'Sylvia's Mother' and listen to the commentary and ...

'So this place is run by her just for money, and she exploits all these poor women with men like you who've no experience of therapy at all?'

'Yes,' mumbles the bloke through a mouthful of soft pink flesh. What a welsher! He's obviously blown it, whatever it is.

As the film ends, and they've cut it heavily to remove some of the naughtier parts – Miss Moone says that she has good news. Unless it's Margaret Thatcher's corsets have become knotted, I cannot imagine what it can be.

And why they have a picture of me up on the screen.

ME!!!!!!!!!!!

That's why the face looked familiar, not to mention any other bits. And why the picture was the same. And the open windows and that funny pendant. Miss Poone/Moone has had me for a sucker. And the clinic is having to close down because of this adverse publicity.

Not that I minded doing a bit of sucking, actually.

So Marilyn has lost Jonny, and her clinic and all that money.

As a cheque arrives in the post next day from the T.V. company for 'Services rendered' and signed by Miss Moone, I shall cry for her all the way to the bank.

And now it's time for me to go. But be of good cheer. And worry not. I promise you that Jonny May will come again.

And again.

And again.

(Publisher's Note: You've only got yourselves to blame. You shouldn't keep buying the damn things!)

I'll leave you with the sort of joke I'd like you to send me.

Man, probably a Publisher, goes to Hell. Having died first. Wonders what it's going to be like. The Devil, who looks strangely like my brother Morrie, offers him three choices.

First one is to be constantly torn to pieces by great vultures with red-hot beaks.

Second choice is to be stretched on a rack, while having to listen to Bay City Rollers' records.

Third choice he's shown is to stand in a vast pool of stinking crap, bubbling and heaving. But he sees that all the men and women who've chosen that are standing there, with the crap only up to their waists, drinking from cups.

That looks the best, so the Publisher picks that one. Joins them in it, and looks around, thinking this isn't really too bad. Not compared with the other horrendous choices.

Just then the Devil appears and shouts out: 'Right. Tea-break's over. Back on your heads!!'

Bye now.

And keep on truckin'.

The Revenger Series from Sphere:

THE GOLD-PLATED HEARSE	Joseph Hedges
THE RAINBOW COLOURED SHROUD	Joseph Hedges
FUNERAL RITES	Joseph Hedges
THE CHINESE COFFIN	Joseph Hedges
ARMS FOR OBLIVION	Joseph Hedges
CORPSE ON ICE	Joseph Hedges
THE MILE DEEP GRAVE	Joseph Hedges
MEXICAN MOURNING	Joseph Hedges
THE STAINLESS STEEL WREATH	Joseph Hedges
THE CHAUFFEUR-DRIVEN PYRE	Joseph Hedges
THE GATES OF DEATH	Joseph Hedges